THE FINAL WALTZ

A Bell Tolls Cosy Mystery

Other Books by Patricia Pike

Air Whisperers of Nkandla

THE FINAL WALTZ

Patricia Pike

A Bell Tolls Cozy Mystery Book 1

Reshwity Publishing
https://reshwity.wixsite.com/publishing

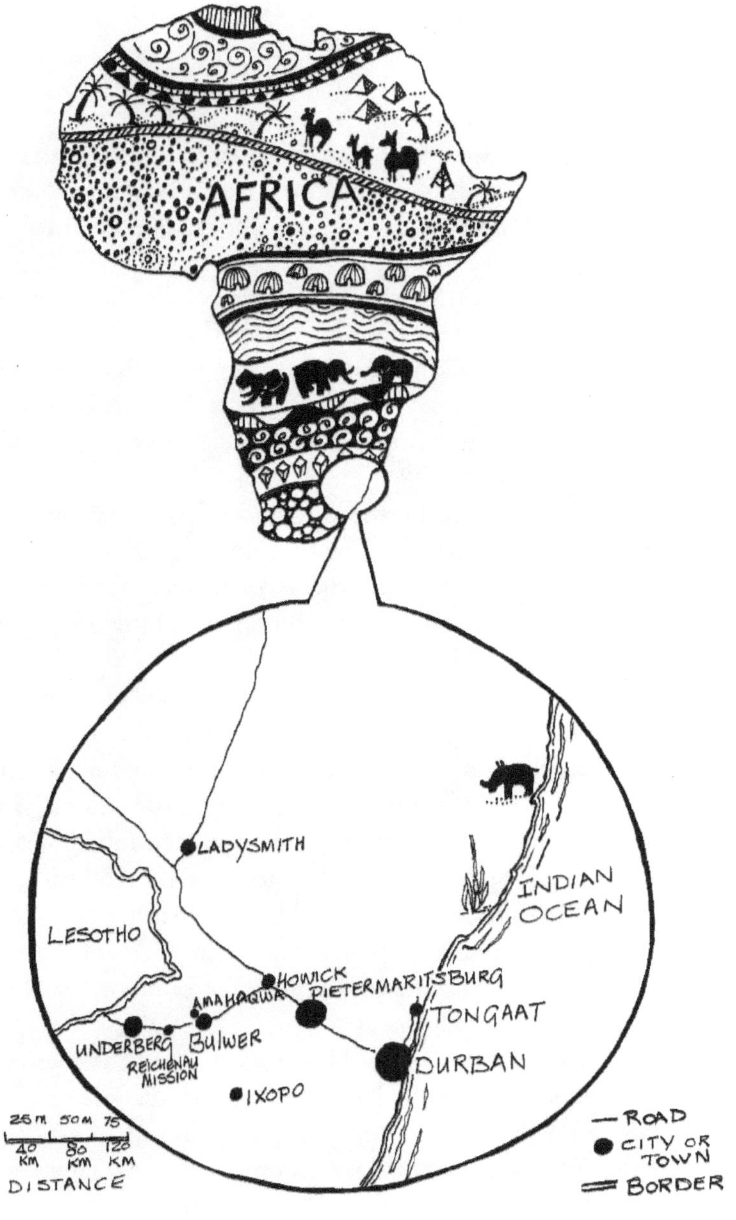

AFRICA
LADYSMITH
LESOTHO
INDIAN OCEAN
HOWICK
AMAHAQWA
PIETERMARITSBURG
TONGAAT
UNDERBERG
Bulwer
REICHENAU MISSION
DURBAN
IXOPO
25M 50M 75
40 KM 80 KM 120 KM
DISTANCE
ROAD
CITY OR TOWN
BORDER

CHAPTER ONE

The young man's footsteps created small puffs of dust as he trudged along the road. Mountains soared to his left and fields of farmland stretched into the distance ahead of him.

A small farm dam offered him a welcome drink of ice cold water. Kneeling he scooped up the water with one hand. He didn't mind that he shared his drinking place with various curious animals and birds. World War two had given him an appreciation of peace and quiet and nature.

He embraced the serenity and hugged it to himself like a precious gift as a he found a spot under a shady tree during the heat of the African day. He woke to find a crow sitting on a branch watching him with intent.

"Come dance with me little bird. Let us celebrate this day," He called to his new companion.

Glancing at his dusty shoes he laughed softly. "Not the right shoes for a jig my little friend. I'm hoping to have new shoes soon and a beautiful girl to hold in my arms as I twirl." The crow blinked his eyes and then took to the sky in search of more comprehensible company. The man threw his arms into the air and did a joyful jig as he contemplated his journey's end.

"Not far now." He called to the empty countryside. A Zulu herd boy in the distance raised his head from his game of Malabalaba in query. But the youngster soon lost interest in him cavorting amongst the fields and went back to his game.

"Bulwer where sadness ends and life begins." He sang off key. "Bulwer named for a Governor and now the home of the most beautiful, sweet woman in the whole wide world." stepping onto the road once more he walked towards the small mountain village with renewed vigour.

The day was almost done when he reached his destination. Zulu women shyly greeted him as he passed the village shops. They sat cross-legged on the pavement selling their homemade wares. Baskets and clay containers butted up against beaded animals, carved wooden knick-knacks, fruit and vegetables, herbs, and spices laid out on grass mats for the customers to choose.

The man did not stop to buy any of these offerings instead he bent down in front of an ancient woman and spoke to her in her own language, "Gogo, could you tell me where to find the Mountain Park Hotel? I have an errand of the heart to complete?"

The old lady offered a toothless smile to his query. "You are close, my son. The hotel is up that roadway and you'll pass a few houses and cross a small stream. You can't miss the hotel. It is large and painted a bright colour." She softly touched his arm and peered into his eyes as she said this.

Thanking her, he followed the direction of her pointing finger. Straightening his jacket he ran his fingers through his army cut, almost non-existent, hair. The old lady shook her head and called out. "The ancestors whisper son. Beware. Tch hamba whena." Her voice dropped so he doubted the last was meant for him. "Hamba."

Chapter Two

The misty mountains of Amahaqwa were a welcome sight to Helen. The old car crested the rise with a puff of smoke from its tailpipe, and turned the corner to reveal the small village of Bulwer nestled under the shadow of Amahaqwa. Not far now.

Her mother, Ada, snored softly in the seat next to her. Mouth open and head resting on the doorframe as the car bumped along. They had left Pietermaritzburg at eleven in the morning and headed north along the partially tar sealed road, past wandering herds of Nguni cattle and grinning young boys endeavouring to drive them to their daily pastures.

They had stopped for a picnic lunch alongside a mountain stream near the road, snacking on Scotch eggs and cucumber sandwiches. The stunning scenery pleased the eye and the heart but three hours of peering through a dusty windscreen had taken its toll and Helen was ready for the journey to end.

Eyes scratchy and sore she knew this travel was essential so she could get the holiday she anticipated. Her shoulders paid the price of gripping the steering wheel for those hours. She felt the slow ache creeping up her neck and into her head that no amount of wriggling would alleviate.

A vague meow from Wisp reminded Helen she was not the only one who was tired of travelling. A cold drink was all Helen could think of as she steered the car off the highway and onto the side road.

Ada woke with a grunt as they went over a rut in the road. A four-storied building rose ahead of them signaled the end of their trip for the day.

Stones shaped by hand gave the building a sound foundation below plastered yellow walls. Roses grew wildly over a wooden pergola leading to the main doors of the hotel. Well-cut lawns stretched across a wide expanse towards ancient trees that harboured rustic seats in amongst gnarled trunks. The floral perfume of roses and lavender wafted through the open windows of the car.

Studying the upper windows Helen hoped the beds were comfortable. A good lie down would sort out her aches and pains in no time. Though she was looking forward to getting out and about. She had been spending too much time lately looking for an escape from pain.

Her mother leaned out the half open door. "So European looking. Very swish. Are those statues? How decadent. And the lead windows are so quaint." Helen watched Ada as her sharp glance surveyed the hotel. Sitting up straighter in her seat she didn't show her own tiredness. It was not often that she got to indulge in her love of architecture and gardens at the same time and Helen had considered that when she had picked their vacation location. She had even studied up on the hotel so she could offer some insight.

"The hotel was built six years ago in 1940 by some Italian prisoners of war. It looked so quaint in the brochure and perfect for a vacation. It's supposed to look old, but it's all up to date with electricity and running water and lots of lovely food and good company." Helen crossed her fingers in the hopes that the hotel would be everything she had dreamed of.

"I'm looking forward to a few days being waited on hand and foot, far from the heat of Zululand, with scenery to sketch and people to meet. Just what I need. Life has been a bit of a nightmare lately." Helen sighed.

Helen suppressed a sigh of fatigue and turned to her mother. "How does a cold drink sound? Maybe they'll have ice-cream or dessert after dinner. So pleasant not to have to decide what to cook." And how nice not to have to feel guilty for having a treat. The war years had been a test for everyone, at home and abroad.

Helen smiled at Ada and it was a smile that spread deep down into her whole being. She held on to the feeling as being enthusiastic about life was a fickle emotion in her current life.

It was marginally cooler outside of the car as Helen unstrapped her trusted bicycle from the back. Too many years of watching every drop of petrol like a hawk during the war and a great love of cycling meant she felt naked without the aged bike. It had lived a previous life as a postman's delivery vehicle and sometimes she thought the front wheel would take off on its own along its old paths.

She patted it fondly as it had kept her sane when she got the news that her fiancé had been killed in Italy. She had gone cycling through the old parts of Pietermaritzburg for hours until finally night had descended and she had returned home to face the fact that David would never come home again.

Wisp had been her solace. When Helen was tired of putting on a happy face or of people asking her if she was okay, she would put Wisp in the postman's basket on the front of the bike and go for a ride until the wind in her hair and the fresh air in her lungs ameliorated the ache in her heart.

They were inseparable, the grey tabby cat and Helen on the bicycle. Wisp loved sitting in the wicker basket or perching on the front of the handlebars as Helen took to the roads. Like a queen surveying her subjects, Wisp allowed the odd tickle of the throat from a besotted admirer. But the car drive had been long and tiresome and she was not feeling kindly toward her human companions and she growled softly as the basket was removed from the back seat of the car. An angry hiss announced the displeasure of its occupant as she was set on the ground.

Helen made sure to bring her in first, out of the heat of the sun. Green eyes peered out at Helen as she walked towards the reception with her mother. They were followed by two Zulu porters who appeared as the women unpacked the car. Dressed in crisp white uniforms that glowed against their ebony black skins, the two men efficiently dealt with the baggage.

Helen noted that neither of them had shoes on their feet and she felt a giggle rise in her chest. The porter with 'Simeon' printed on his uniform must have discerned what had instigated the mirth as he wiggled his toes and grinned when Helen burst into a guffaw.

Ada frowned. "Helen, enough unseemly hilarity. Let's go inside."

Her mother's need for manners didn't have room for mirth. Helen pretended to be shamefaced, but still grinned from ear to ear. The path lead towards a sign that said 'Reception'.

The cool stone of the hotel engulfed her and eased part of the headache. She shuddered as the temperature drop turned the sweat from the drive to ice down her spine. Reception was made of a large edifice of wood with small hooks behind it holding shiny brass keys.

Helen tapped the bell on the front desk and the sound reverberated through the foyer. "Loud enough to wake the dead." She muttered under her breath and then shivered slightly as a cold wind slid down her back. What is that all about?

Helen straightened as a woman breezed through from the kitchen. The hiss of boiling water was over powered by the crack of knives on cutting boards. The door closed, dampening the noise to a soft hum.

All business, the booking ledger was flipped open. Glasses adjusted on a pert little nose and the receptionist confirmed their reservation. "Welcome to the Mountain Park Hotel. I trust your travel here was not too arduous? Let me get the porters to see to your luggage and then we can complete the formalities."

Her name tag sat perfectly straight on her lapel. She had the most amazing red hair Helen had ever seen. A gold capped tooth winked at her as she watched the two porters handle the awkward luggage.

The receptionist eyed the bicycle and pointed to a storage cupboard beneath the stairs. "Simeon, the bike should fit in nicely if you move Mr. Sam's canoe into the corner. Sipho, I'm sure you can manage a cat basket and a suitcase in one go. They don't look too heavy."

Having given the staff their instructions she turned towards her two guests. Her eyes sparkled with love of life and Helen couldn't help smiling back.

"We do not stand on ceremony at the Mountain Park Hotel, so call me Charlotte, I'm sure by the end of your stay we'll be firm friends, so why not start as we mean to continue."

The smile was all too familiar. It was only as she spoke that Helen was able to dig out of her memory the connection. "I know you. Didn't you go to St Cuthbert's in Durban North?" Helen had not particularly liked school so most of her memories of the time were vague except for the few kindnesses shown.

"I think you were a year or so ahead of me? I was a junior and you were a senior. Yes, I'm sure. 1928 I was a scared young schoolgirl far from home and you were kind to me. You gave me some biscuits the first night I was there. Wow, isn't this just so amazing? To meet up all these years later."

Surprise widened Charlotte's eyes. "You have the most incredible memory, Helen. I can barely remember our school years. St Cuthbert's seems like a million years away. I only stayed two years and then had to go home to help my aunt. Money was always a problem at home and I started work at a small hotel. I'm amazed you recognised me with this hair. The last time we met I was a mousy brown colour. We must get together some time and catch up. But let me show you your rooms first. We have plenty of time."

Helen felt another cold shiver down her back at this statement. She recognised the feeling but she wasn't about to entertain what it could mean.

Charlotte hopped up from her chair behind the desk with agility and displayed heels of impressive height. She moved like she was dancing to silent music and chatted as she took another set of keys from the wall behind the reception desk. Walking towards the stairs ahead of them she motioned for them to follow her. Helen was in awe of her balancing act on the precarious heels and her amazing skills at not missing a step as she navigated the carpet covered stairs at speed.

"This way to your rooms, ladies. Gee Helen, it's fabulous that you recognised me. I'm sure I must have changed a lot since we last met and not just the hair. I was called Lottie at school, of course there were other nicknames, not so pleasant." She laughed softly though Helen could hear the old bitterness. Helen wasn't the only one who hadn't fit in at school.

Helen paused to help her mother up the last few steps. At the top of the stairs Charlotte pointed to the right and continued on. "The bathroom is down the hall a little way, but the other guests are all lovely and you'll have no problems using the facilities with privacy. Aah, here we are. This one is for you Helen and this larger one for Mrs. Bell." Charlotte threw open the two doors and spread her arms wide, encouraging them to admire the appointments.

Helen's room had a pretty dusty pink spread on the bed and two small bed side tables either side with lamps on them. The lamps were decorated with delicate sprays of china flowers covered with tiny butterflies on paper thin ceramic bases and topped with a lacy shade and looked extremely fragile. Helen hoped Wisp would not be tempted to jump up on the tables and damage the pretty lamps. Butterfly prints on the walls and soft cushions in pastel completed the décor.

Ada's room was almost double the size of Helen's and apart from a much larger bed, had an antique desk and a comfy couch. The furniture looked as if it had been transported from a very fancy French chateau. Spindle legs on the desk spoke of workmanship of a bygone era and the couch was covered in pale green striped silk and adorned with scattered cushions of exotic hues pleasing to the eye.

Helen ran her fingers over the silken smooth desk top and picked up a cushion just to enjoy its texture while she waited for her mother to finish her own perusal of the rooms.

Bowls of potpourri scented the room with the perfume of a thousand roses and other yet undiscovered floral delights.

"Yes, this will do," said Ada as she walked briskly across the room to peer out of the window at the manicured lawns below her. "This will suit me nicely it is quite lovely. Thank you, Charlotte."

A chamber maid as dark as ebony, popped her head around the door. "Tea is being served in the lounge. I'll unpack for you while you are away." She smoothed a hand down a crisp white apron over a green and white uniform as she spoke. She smiled and they were dazzled by the brilliant white teeth that were exposed. Her eyes sparkled with youth and interest as she bent and opened the door to the cat cage.

Wisp wound herself around the young woman's legs in pleasure at finally being free of her confines.

"My name is Delphinia and I'll be at your service during your stay. Ask me for anything and I will see if it is available," She said as she placed clean towels on the foot of the bed, topped with a glorious red gold bar of Pears soap.

Helen couldn't refrain from picking the soap up and sniffing it as the young woman smoothed the covers and then turned to leave. She called over her shoulder. "Leave your cases to me, Madam. I'll unpack them for you in a jiffy."

Charlotte smiled and returned to her duties with a promise they would catch up later.

Helen and Ada tidied themselves up quickly in preparation for hotel life. A quick brush of the hair, a dab of perfume and lipstick and a change of clothing and they were ready. Wisp observed this procedure with interest as she licked her paws and attended to her own ablutions. She pranced ahead of them out of the door and down the stairs, probably determined not to miss a moment of this new experience.

The lounge was almost full by the time Helen and her mother descended the stairs. Overstuffed chairs covered in a rich green velvet and trimmed in gold gleamed in the light of lamps scattered around the room. The windows were the mullioned windows they had noticed on their arrival and had layers of lace and scarlet silk curtains lavishly falling on each side and excluded the bulk of the daylight from entering the room.

Impressive lamps cast puddles of light amongst the gloom and a large man with a huge handlebar moustache sat next to a tiny mouse of a woman in one such puddle. The rest of the room was inhabited by women of various ages who all looked up at their arrival. Charlotte was already there and linked her hand through Helen's arm as she introduced them all, breezing in with a wave of her hand and a flick of her hair. Her high heels barely made a sound on the thick carpeting as she approached and clapped her hands to gain everyone's attention.

"Guests. This is Helen and Ada Bell. Old friends from a long time ago. This lovely gentleman is Major Swindells-Smythe and his dear wife, Maisie." The major raised himself to greet them, and Maisie jumped up to pump their hands in welcome. The major's moustache quivered slightly as he bobbed his head towards the new arrivals.

"New faces. Let me guess. Mother and daughter — or sisters. You look so much alike, both pretty," Maisie gushed. Helen smiled at the thought Ada might be her sister. Helen could see that her mother was greatly flattered by this statement and was smiling kindly on the mouse like Maisie.

Maisie tucked an errant grey curl behind her ear as she patted the seat next to her in invitation for Ada to join her. Her pale beige dress and pink cardigan melted into the shadows as Ada settled herself.

Charlotte continued with her introductions. "Miss Ruth Ferris is a governess to the daughter of our hotel manager, Mr. van Rooyen. Mathilda, the daughter, is not here today. Her Momma has taken her to the city to the doctors." Charlotte nodded her head towards a woman with a smart grey suit reading a book in the corner. Ruth looked up momentarily and smiled in a distracted way.

"Pamela Meaker, retired secretary to Winston Churchill and newly arrived in our area with the desire to find accommodation." Pamela lifted her cup of tea toward them in a silent salute. She was the epitome of a stalwart British woman. Her walking shoes were practical and sturdy and her clothes of finely tailored tweed looked slightly out of place in Africa.

The strange caterpillar brooch looked odd on such a staid lady and Helen wondered if it might have some sentimental meaning.

"Fiona Ferris, and yes, they are sisters." Fiona had a luxuriant head of blonde hair that glowed in the lamplight. Gold earrings and an impressive array of expensive jewellery competed with the vision that was Fiona Ferris. If they had not been informed of the relationship Helen would have never thought that the grey suited Ruth and the flashy Fiona were connected in a familial way. Fiona wore her hair styled along with an equally fashionable outfit of maroon trimmed with white and looked very different to her grey suited sister. She looked like she had just stepped out of the pages of a fashion magazine.

Charlotte flicked her wrist at Ruth, who smiled in agreement. "And finally, Susanna, or as we like to call her, Sue Van der Merwe our resident travelling district nurse. Always handy with a plaster or a pill or lotion if needed."

Sue, the nurse, wore a uniform, obviously medical in origin as one pocket sported a thermometer and a stethoscope peeped out of another pocket. Helen felt a quick affinity to Sue as she was reminded of all those days her father, the doctor, had allowed her to join him on his rounds.

Helen smiled at everyone and she wondered if her cheeks would be aching with all this unaccustomed grinning at people by the end of the day. "Glad to meet you all. My mother and I are looking forward to getting to know you all."

With her short introduction Charlotte was able to make them feel relaxed with each other and Ada chatted with Maisie, while Helen sat next to Fiona. Charlotte sashayed across the floor and back to her desk. Helen was glad she had made the effort to break the ice between all the guests.

"Charlotte told us what everyone else does, but she seems to have neglected you. Can I be so bold as to ask what your interest is?" Helen asked as she settled on one of the comfy chairs next to Fiona.

Fiona leaned back in her chair and with a nervous giggle said, "Well, I don't actually do much at all. I was engaged to Edward McCarthy, the heir to the chocolate millions. Sadly, he was killed in the first weeks of the war at Dunkirk. But he left a will in my favour. Can't say I'm popular with his parents and siblings, but they're happy to pay me a dividend as long as I keep myself out of good society and out in the countryside. And this is as country as it gets." She sipped her black tea and declined the sweet treats on offer. Helen with a bubble of glee picked out her favourite from the tray offered and flashed a smile to the server.

A hot cup of tea with extra cream and a small angel cake in her hands, Helen did something she didn't do very often. She spoke about herself.

"I was engaged to a soldier too. He wasn't rich or anyone important, well except he was my whole life to me. A rogue gunman shot him as he walked in the hills on his leave day in Italy." Helen remembered the emotional half written letter telling her all about the beauty of the country and the friendliness of the people. A letter enclosed within another one written by his commanding officer with the news that David would not be completing his letter or returning to South Africa.

Helen contemplated her hands around the cup of tea. Six months ago they would have shook. It seemed time did heal wounds. "It seems strange to think of him alive one moment and dead the next. Sorry. I'm telling you this and we have barely met. What will you think of me?"

She blinked the tears from her eyes. So much for time healing her wounds. She had finished crying her tears for David months ago. Helen took a deep breath and smiled weakly.

Fiona patted her hand and Pamela Meaker got abruptly to her feet and rushed out of the room holding a handkerchief to her face as tears made their way down her cheeks. War affected everyone, even the secretaries of Winston Churchill it seemed.

Helen leaned over to Maisie and asked, "Is she okay? I hope it wasn't anything I said or did that caused her grief."

"Oh no dear," Maisie replied. "Did you notice that strange pin she was wearing that is shaped like a caterpillar?" At Helen's positive nod Maisie continued. "Her only brother was flying in a plane heading for Greece on a secret mission, when they were shot by enemy fire. He managed to wriggle out and use his parachute to land safely. The caterpillar is a club that honours people who have escaped unhurt from damaged aircraft. Sadly he died later in the war. She finds the death of young men especially emotional as she remembers her own brother. She will go and have a good cry and be right as rain in no time at all. Don't worry my dear you could not have known how fragile she is. Don't mention the caterpillar club and you will be fine."

Helen nodded in sympathy and turned back to listen to the other conversations in the lounge. The nurse was sitting up straight in her seat as she smoothed down her clothing and then leaned over to say, "There is a serious lack of eligible young men after the war and women need to get on and develop a life for themselves. Look at me. I earn a good wage and am my own boss most of the time. A few reports to head office and sometimes a review by a senior nurse. But I love it. Who needs a man in their life? Not me."

Sue had a severe face that resembled a chisel and eyes like they were made of flint and had never smiled in their short acquaintance. "I am happy on my own thank you very much. Ya nee, men just bring pain and heartache." Her false bravado fooled no one. Helen wondered if she too had lost someone in the war.

Sue purposefully raised her feet onto the footstool and glared at the other ladies around her.

Poor David, lying dead in the prime of his life and all those other soldiers that would never return home. Helen wished he was here beside her. Rather than her trying to cope on her own while others were happy in their relationships.

Her future consisted of hours behind a desk keeping the books for her brother and brother-in-law. And now the job was in jeopardy. The previous bookkeeper had returned from the war and had a family to support. He was eager to resume his former job and Helen could not blame him for ousting her. Helen had told her mother she was using all her vacation time but the truth was she had no job to return to.

Sue might have the right idea. Be more independent. Support herself financially.

Out the corner of her eye, Helen saw a furry grey shadow dart under a sideboard. She peered through the gloom of the large room trying to see what had caused Wisp to invade the lounge and what had excited her hunting instincts. Her tail flicked and a paw emerged from under the furniture as she crept forward. A sudden pounce and the fleet footed cat had its prey.

A few bumps and a high-pitched squeak announced the successful conclusion of a rat hunt. Maisie yelped as Wisp appeared and proudly revealed the still twitching body of a rather large rat. Wisp threw the victim up in the air a few times, twisting and turning in spectacular fashion and then, losing interest in displaying its prowess and the lack of response of her prey, she deposited her prize at Helen's feet.

Helen stood and was just about to take her cat by the scruff of its neck and the rat by its now flaccid tail, when the major heaved himself out of his chair and announced. "Leave the beast to me, little lady. I will sort out the carcass in a jiffy. Clever cat you have there. Excellent mouser."

Taking a sip of his brandy, he straightened his shoulders and twirled his moustache. Grabbing the rat by the tail he marched out of the room and could be heard instructing Simeon on the art of rat disposal in a loud voice reminiscent of a sergeant major on a battle field. "It's nothing to be scared of man, just a dead rat. Here take it and go and bury it in the garden somewhere. Preferably not close to the hotel or where it might be unearthed by another animal. Good man. That is the ticket."

Wisp was not pleased that her prize had been spirited away and glared at Helen. "Wisp you are a challenge sometimes. That nice man is getting rid of the evidence of your killing spree and you need to thank him, not growl at him."

Sue and Ruth had both risen to watch the rat's demise and its expulsion. Wisp sat preening herself in the centre of a Persian rug of obvious antiquity and quality while Mr. van Rooyen, the hotel manager, observed the whole episode from the door of his office and now eyed the feline at the centre of the drama.

"Thank you, Miss Bell for the use of your cat to help assist in the control of our pest problem. Perhaps we can encourage the cat to pursue these hunts somewhere other than the lounge in future?" Wisp looked up at the man and disregarded him as being unimportant in the grand scheme of things and continued with her preening.

Helen quickly picked her cat up and took her outside. Throwing an apologetic grin over her shoulder at Mr. van Rooyen. Fiona, Sue and Ruth followed Helen outdoors and took turns in cuddling Wisp. Helen had to laugh as the ferocious hunter transformed into a soft and cute pet. "Enough of your antics for today, Wisp. Time for you to learn your place. And the place you need to be at the moment is back in the room I think."

Bidding her new acquaintances, a quick farewell, she poked her head into the lounge and informed her mother she would be going to the room to rest, taking her cat with her. The long drive over the dusty roads had been tiring even for a thirty-year-old woman.

CHAPTER THREE

Helen took a nap and was woken to the dinner bell's tones at six pm. She was surprised to realise how hungry she was. Changing into more formal attire, she went down to the dining room eager to see what was on the menu. Meeting her mother on the stairs they went in to dinner together.

The women they had met earlier were interspersed with people they were yet to become acquainted with. The room buzzed with conversation as they walked in. Men in various forms of work dress sat at every table and for a moment Helen didn't know where to sit. Charlotte appeared at their elbow and quickly ushered them to a table with Fiona and two men.

Both men had roughened hands and their handshakes were firm as they introduced themselves.

The younger of the men jumped up to pull out the chairs for the women.

"Samuel. But just call me Sam. I work on the crew building the jail on the hill. This is Steve, my boss." Sam was the younger by a few years than his boss and had a blonde crew cut hair style. His clothes were clean but well worn. The grey checked shirt and black trousers were obviously his Sunday best.

Steve too wore clean and smart clothes but hadn't risen while the women were seated. His blue and white pin striped shirt was crisply ironed and he had taken the time to have his shoes shone to a high gloss.

He nodded as the women were seated and greeted them with a mumbled, "Hello."

Ada was quite at home chatting to these total strangers and as the meal progressed they found out about a wife and children, money and mates. Helen was content to sit back and listen as the conversation flowed around her.

Sam, young and enthusiastic about rugby and pretty girls, while his boss, Steve, missed his wife and children.

Fiona fiddled with her food and allowed the newcomers to dominate the conversation. She had most likely heard the men's stories a hundred times and every so often would add a few comments. She was extremely funny and teased young Sam mercilessly.

"Sammie, who could resist those baby blue eyes? You are such a little baby, any woman would want to cuddle you. As to you Steve, well you are a dark horse. I never knew you missed your wife and kiddies so much. You haven't been home for months. If you really felt homesick for the family you would have been high tailing it over the mountains every opportunity you got."

Steve frowned at Fiona and she smiled sweetly back at him.

Steve rumbled, "You know, when I get home after a stay away, I am thrilled to have the kids climb all over me. But after a week or two, I am eager to go to the next job. I honestly think my wife is happy when I leave, because then she can get back a little bit of control with the youngsters. She lives near her parents and they are a big help when needed. Little blighters give my wife a right royal time of it. They are good kids. Great at sports, but not so good with schooling.

Its prize giving in a few weeks and I think I might just take a few days off to go and cheer them on."

Steve sat back and tapped his stomach. "Wife will have to work hard to beat this grub though. First rate meals. Better than some hotels I have stayed at."

He laughed in a low rumbling guffaw, rising from his feet and shook his whole body. "And, certainly better than army grub. Glad to be home in sunny South Africa. Very glad."

"Aah Steve, if you are going to the big smoke to the prize giving, what about giving the rest of us the day off too? You know we won't do things right if you are not there to check on us every two minutes." Sam queried of his boss.

"No, Sam. You're paid to work, not slack off and visit girls at the drop of a hat," Steve replied with a frown. "Don't you dare encourage the workers to make my life difficult. I know you like to think they are all your mates but just remember I am the boss and don't forget it." Steve scowled at Fiona as she opened her mouth to say something sarcastic and she raised her eyebrows slightly as she closed her mouth once more.

Helen smiled at young Sam and his honesty. He shrugged off his boss' denial of his request with bonhomie and a cheeky grin, not in the least concerned at the reprimand delivered by Steve or the teasing by Fiona.

Helen finished off her trout meal with the steamed vegetables and mashed potatoes. Steve was right. The food was excellent. She had been correct, dessert was served with a large dollop of ice-cream and real cream to top it all off. Ada chose the apple pie and cream, while Helen was tempted by the chocolate mousse.

The Second World War had finished in September and here they were in April, just a few months later, and life and food were slowly returning to normal. Or better than normal in this case.

After dinner, Ada said she would chat to the major and Maisie. "Helen you go and spend time with some people your own age for a change. I will be fine with Maisie. She seems very nice and I am sure we will have plenty to talk about."

Pamela joined the two older ladies and the three of them went through their lists of family and friends to see if the other two knew any of them as they wandered off.

Helen had to laugh as Pamela said, "You live in Pietermaritzburg don't you? I know a woman who moved there after the war. Sarah Fisher. Have you met her? She's a school teacher."

Helen wondered why strangers always imagined that South Africa was such an insular population that everyone knew everyone else. She found it very amusing how often people asked her if she knew some obscure person just because they lived in the same city.

Helen was glad to notice that Pamela was no longer looking teary eyed and seemed happy and pleasant. Helen left her mother in the capable hands of the two new friends and went in pursuit of conversations that did not include tips on sewing and housekeeping.

Helen joined the younger crowd in the ladies' lounge downstairs. Samuel and some of the other men challenged them to a game of pool.

Fiona threw up her hands and said, "Challenge accepted boys. Helen and I will wipe the floor with you. We are both exceptional players and you will regret this night. For all eternity you will be known as the boys whipped into shape by Fiona and Helen, champions of the stick and ball."

Helen looked in surprise at Fiona and whispered, "Fiona, I have never played pool and I rather think we might be out classed. These men look like they know their way around a stick and ball or two."

"It's just strategy, Helen. We need them to think we are better than we are. I myself am useless at these games but I do know a thing or two about men and their egos," Fiona whispered back. "I love a bit of fun to end off the day and this will do the trick nicely thank you. Come along you will enjoy it." She urged Helen.

Much laughter followed as Fiona and Helen both showed themselves unskilled at the game. Helen did manage to sink a ball but it was apparently the wrong one. Feeling pleased with her skill, she was soon told that what she had done was sink the black and it was a bad thing. "I was trying to get you men to relax before we annihilate you. Isn't that right Fiona?"

"Oh, certainmont mon ami." Fiona laughed back at Helen. She whirled around so that her lacy dress formed a perfect circle and had all the men mesmerised by glimpses of a saucy suspender holding up sheer stockings. Her long legs performed an impromptu dance and Helen's gaffe was soon forgotten as the men focused their attention on the feminine form of fun loving Fiona.

"Where is this promised prowess, girlies?" Johan crowed. "Stick and ball is not your forte but there are some things I can think of that you might excel at.

Come with me for an hour and I will educate you in your true talent."

"An hour? Really Johan? I think you are over-estimating your endurance. And no, we have no interest in learning the arts you are wanting to teach us. We are ladies of honour and not your usual fare of ladies of the night. Now let us continue and we will see if Helen and I can recoup our losses," Fiona retaliated.

Johan blushed a deep red and apologised for his faux pas. "Sorry ladies. You're right. I had no right to denigrate you just because you do not know one end of a pool cue from the other. Let me make it up to you. I will cover my one eye to give you an advantage during this next game. Fair?"

No matter the things the men did to give the women the advantage, the women were not able to overcome their natural prowess at the game. The men moved on from ice cold beers to whisky and their skill suffered as a result.

When they suggested they change games and play darts, both girls declined their offer and left them to it. Helen called it a night.

Helen noticed Steve leaning over the reception desk and whispering in Charlotte's ear. He blushed a bright red and said loudly, "My key please Charlotte. Oh, hi there Miss Bell. I hope you had a pleasant evening. I had better get back to my workers and make sure they all get to bed at a decent hour. It feels like I have a dozen children to look after and not just a building project." He smiled and turned towards the pub door waving at the two women in the reception area.

Charlotte smiled at Helen. Helen took that as a sign that Charlotte wanted to talk and replaced Steve at the desk. Charlotte shifted the few items on the immaculate desk as she said, "The memories are coming back about those school years. And not all of them pleasant either. The girls in the group of bullies gave you the nickname of Helen the Cretin. I thought it was quite imaginative for them. Their usual selection was things like Snotty Lottie and Potty faced Lottie. Each week was some new abuse dreamed up by Abigail Olifant and her gang of equally idiotic girls. Did you hear what happened to the ringleader, Abigail? She runs a brothel on Point road. I nearly laughed myself silly when I heard about it."

"Oh Lottie, you have an amazing memory. I try to blot out all those nasty things from school. I heard about Abigail and must admit to a bit of surprise at her choice of career. Then I heard her Mom was a prostitute and had paid for her fancy schooling by servicing the men at the docks. I know I shouldn't take any joy in her sad life, but after what she put us through, well I did smile just a little bit."

Helen and Charlotte laughed softly together for a moment. "Well, better get on and get my Mom to bed and stop gossiping like an air head. Night Charlotte. Hope you have a good sleep. See you tomorrow and we can really catch up," Helen said as she turned to go.

The major and Maisie were in the lounge with Ada. Apparently, the steps down to the pub scared Maisie as she stated in a slightly too loud voice, "I feel a shiver go down my spine each time I walk down the pub lounge stairs. I even thought I heard someone crying last week, but there was no one there. The major really doesn't care where he drinks as long as someone fills his glass every once in a while. So, we spend our evenings here in the lounge and we are both happier."

Maisie looked up when Helen approached them. "Aah are you here to take your Mom off to bed? What a sensible, lovely daughter you are. Wish my bunch were half as thoughtful."

The major harrumphed in agreement and levered himself out of the soft chair. "Time for us to be hitting the sack, old girl. Here let me give you a hand."

He wobbled slightly on his legs and Helen watched with concern as the two-elderly people wove their way to the stairs and hopefully a good night's rest. The Major and Maisie had both changed for dinner and Helen smiled as she wondered where Maisie had purchased her Chinese cheongsam dress with its exotic embroidery. They looked rather resplendent together. Him with his uniform and her with her dress fashioned in a faraway country.

Once upstairs the noise from the pub was muted and Helen were able to sink into their pillows and were soon fast asleep. Helen cuddled into Wisp in her luxurious bed.

The corridors might have been dimly lit, but the furtive movements of people were just visible if Helen looked carefully into the shadows. Whispers floated on the night as moonbeams danced as sleep claimed her.

CHAPTER FOUR

Constable Gordon Brown muttered under his breath as he stumbled through his home. He knocked the phone off the wall before he gathered his wits enough to prop it against his ear. The words took a long time to turn into a sentence.

A dead woman at a hotel.

He tried twice before he put the phone back on its hook. By the time he had his shower and was straddling his motorbike he was sufficiently awake to make the trip.

Constable Brown traversed the dusty country road up the mountainous passes from Pietermaritzburg, avoiding potholes and wandering cattle in pursuit of his duty. He was able to make good time and arrived as day was breaking over the African countryside having driven through most of the night.

Hands frozen in the chill morning mist and from hours of gripping handle bars, it took a large mug of steaming hot coffee to thaw him out. Some kind person had lit the fire in the lounge at the hotel and Cook brought him a plate of toast and marmalade, Gordon smiled as he gratefully gobbled it down.

His face dusty and grimy from dead insects and dust had encrusted his skin. He doubted he instilled any confidence of his qualifications as a Constable to the staff and yet they treated him as an important guest. With the tools he had on hand he washed his face as much as he could. Dusting off his uniform in a vain hope the stain of travel would not be too obvious. And then he was ready to face the tasks of the day.

Sue arrived with tear filled eyes to escort him upstairs. Gordon shook her hand, as Mr. van Rooyen patted her back in a comforting way. "This is the lady who discovered the body, Constable. She is a nurse and used to death, but this was very shocking for a young lady to deal with." Mr. van Rooyen informed him.

Sue looked at the men through red rimmed eyes puffy from lack of sleep or too much crying.

"Thank you Mr. van Rooyen, it was awful. I think it's because I knew Charlotte so well." She looked at the constable and the tears started flowing once more as she said, "She was full of the love of life. Always smiling, always kind." Brushing away more tears, she said, "Let me take you to her. She is in her room on her bed, she looks so peaceful now."

Mr. van Rooyen fussed with the cuffs of his jacket. "No complaining about moving her. She was on the stairs and the guests would have been upset. Deplorable the state she was in. The guests, you understand, would not stand for it."

Gordon ignored his defensiveness and reassured him, "I'm sure it will be fine. You can show me where she was found. Anything else you can tell me?"

Sue turned to Mr. van Rooyen and with a catch in her voice said, "There are things in this hotel I find very strange. Windows open on their own and even the taps switch themselves on in the bathrooms. All the staff have seen something they are scared to talk about, but never a death. Charlotte said she was scared to walk alone along the top passageway. I didn't believe her then, but now, I think she might have known something."

Mr. van Rooyen shook his head at Sue being so fanciful and patted her arm once more in sympathy. "Ag nee. Ghosts have no part in Charlotte's death. She was just unfortunate and I always told her those high heels would be the death of her one day. That carpet was loose. I told them to fix it but I never thought it would lead to this. I blame the shoes. No one else has tripped over the carpet before. But she refused to change them for something more sensible. She said they reminded her of the times she participated in dance competitions. Poor girl will never dance again."

Sniffing into her large man's handkerchief Sue led the way up the stairs to the top floor. She gingerly opened the door to Charlotte's bedroom and stood back. The first thing Gordon noted was Charlotte wore very high heels and a rather revealing outfit fitting tightly over her ample frame.

Sue shivered slightly as she whispered, "She seemed to fall from nowhere. I was just about to walk up the stairs when I saw a blue object come rolling down the stairs. She looked like a ragdoll. Arms and legs falling everywhere and it was only when she landed at my feet I knew it was a person. Poor Charlotte. It was so quick but it felt like it was all moving so slowly."

She sniffed loudly into her handkerchief. "I know there is a ghost here somewhere in the hotel. I have seen something white on the stairs when I get back late at night, which I do quite often. I go to see Mr. Page down the road at eleven at night to give him his final medication for the day. When I get back there is a feeling of someone watching me when I walk up the stairs. There is no one around, but I always carry a torch for protection and in case the lights are out."

She shrugged her shoulders as if to apologise. "I'm a sensible Boer girl, Constable. Not given to fanciful stuff at all. I have not mentioned this to anyone before and I would appreciate it you didn't share my confidence with anyone else, but it might be important, somehow. Maybe she saw something and was distracted and didn't see the carpet? I don't know how, oh just forget I said anything about ghosts. It is just my imagination." Sue seemed upset and her hands shook slightly as she straightened her skirt and then twisted her fingers together.

Gordon smiled at her in a kind way, not knowing what else to do to sooth her feelings. Sue twisted the soggy handkerchief in her hands and blew her nose noisily as she rose from the end of the bed and prepared to leave. She patted Charlotte's leg in a consolatory fashion and walked out glancing back as she reached the door.

"If you need me to make a statement I will be back from my rounds at about twelve." Gordon jotted down a few salient facts as she spoke. He nodded at her. It would be better to get her statement once she was a little less emotional.

The large handkerchief was no match for Sue's tears and she started searching through her pockets for a clean replacement. Sniffing loudly she made her way out the door and down the stairs.

Gordon waited for Sue to leave before examining the corpse closely. He closed the door firmly and then stood back to observe the young woman in front of him. Taking a deep breath, he started at her head and gently twisted her head to the side.

A large gash on the back of the head was a concern and he would need to look at the bannister along her path of descent. He sat down next to her bed and took out his notebook to take notes.

Once he had noted carefully what he found he continued with his examination. Her legs and body were all as they should be and he carefully pulled her clothes back into a semblance of modesty.

Mr. van Rooyen had said the doctor would only be able to visit later in the morning and there was not much more he could do in the interim. He decided not to leave the body alone for no good reason.

There was the nasty gash on the back of the head, but no sign of foul play. So why did he feel the need to stay close at hand. He had a long wait ahead of him as he sat in expectation of a medical doctor to sign his little bit of paper so he could return to the city.

Death was an inconvenience, especially for someone young and as pretty as Charlotte.

Gordon was not a stranger to death during the war and this reminded him of David and Helen, his best friends from childhood. Six months might not seem long to some people, but for Helen he knew her grief had been intense since David died.

They had grown up together and David had been a larger than life character, dominating everything they did. From using rafts of logs to travel down the Umzimduzi river in the aftermath of a rain storm, to David's proposal to Helen with a guitar playing a serenade under her window and the antique engagement ring.

Gordon had been an interested observer of this romance between his two best friends and now an observer of the grief of Helen as she dealt with the aftermath. Many a night she had looked for relief on Gordon's shoulder, she had looked lost and alone in a bubble of hurt and pain. His heart ached for her but he had no idea how to alleviate her angst in any way.

He was sure he had heard the meow of Wisp her cat as he walked up the stairs, but he knew it just couldn't be. A figment of his imagination perhaps? Hadn't Sue the nurse mentioned ghosts? He smiled to himself as he thought he had never heard of a cat ghost.

Gordon shook his head as if to shake off his imagining of pretty girls and cats far away. He took out his notepad and did one final walk around the body before sitting down at the head of the bed in an attitude of protecting the victim.

CHAPTER FIVE

Helen walked through the rose garden with her cat in the morning mist when Johan approached. He was a rather handsome man of about thirty years of age and had been ogling Helen the evening before. He took this opportunity to follow her outside to get her alone.

He matched his pace to walk with her. "Now, Helen sweetheart, if there is anything, and I mean anything I can do for you, just give me a call. I have been assigned by Heaven to watch over their angels."

Helen laughed. "Oh Johan, you are a smooth talker. But you go back to your darts game and I'll will be quite able to cope on my own."

He leaned over and gave her a quick peck on the cheek before saying, "Heaven is a little less beautiful today because you have graced us with your presence. If I told you had a beautiful body, would you hold it against me? And I'm sorry I was so crass last night. You are truly a class act and I promise to behave from now on." Johan quipped with a quick smile bringing out the dimples in his chin and cheeks.

Helen was amused by his flirting but it fell on an empty heart. "Sorry Johan, but this angel has a bit too much of the devil in her to fall for that old line of charm. My Granma always said that a man with a dimple in his chin has the devil within. And you have more than your fair share of dimples and who knows if you have a devil within? Off you go, saucy man." Helen patted his hand. He laughed as he strode back to the hotel.

Wisp was not happy with the attention Helen received and spat and hissed. Helen picked her up and cuddled into her while she watched the young man walk away towards work until the mist blurred his outline and swallowed him up in its tendrils.

After her walk in the garden, Helen sat in her room sipping on a cup of piping hot tea and stroked Wisp absentmindedly. She had the strangest feeling something wasn't right. A vague memory of Charlotte sitting on her bed in the middle of the night, weeping and sighing. But it hadn't felt real.

Helen frowned as she remembered the voice of her friend Gordon drift into her dreams and she wondered how he was enjoying his new career in the police. Gordon who had changed from a gangly youth to a kind and gentle adult without anyone even noticing the changes. Who would have thought the boy with ears sticking out like windmills, would one day look so handsome? As she pondered on this thought, Delphinia knocked on the door.

"Miss Bell, breakfast might be a little bit late today. Miss Charlotte had an accident last night and is not there to organise things. I apologise. You have a nice hot bath and take your time and breakfast will be served soon."

Before Helen could ask Delphinia if Miss Charlotte was okay, the young girl was gone. Helen drank her tea and had a hot bath before knocking on her mother's door. "Mom, are you up yet?"

"Come in, Helen. Yes, I'm up and bathed and even dressed for the day. A bit of mist out there, but we should be able to climb Amahaqwa and see the rock paintings if we have a quick bite to eat. I asked the cook to make us up a small hamper to take with us in case the climb is longer than anticipated.”

“But what about Charlotte? Did you hear she had an accident?” Helen asked.

“Oh yes, but I’m sure she will be fine. Maybe a few days off work will see her right. You will be able to chat as much as you like. Catch up on all the news of school friends. Now come along, no time for malingering,” Ada answered.

“Mom, I really feel we should pop in to see the poor girl first, before dashing off to the wide blue yonder. I just feel it in my bones something is not right. Five minutes won’t hurt us. Come along, the climb up the stairs will be a warm you up for your mountain hike and I will feel better knowing she is being looked after,” Helen cajoled her mother.

Ada sighed and said, “Oh okay, but it will just be a waste of time. She is most probably enjoying a nice lie in and being waited on hand and foot by little Delphinia.”

It was obvious which door belonged to Charlotte as it had a plaque hanging on the non-descript door saying “Charlotte” with wooden painted hearts surrounding it. Helen knocked on the bedroom door and without waiting for a reply, opened it and stepped inside.

“Gordon. What the heck are you doing here sitting next to Charlotte’s bed?” Helen glared at him. He looked overly comfortable in the chair.

“Helen?”

“And what is wrong with Charlotte? I thought it was a simple accident and not something to concern the police? Mom, come in, look who is here? Gordon all the way up here in the mountains far from home. I told you there was something wrong, and it's as wrong as it can be." Helen didn't want to analyse the jealousy that wrapped around her seeing Gordon in a woman's room.

"Helen, shush. You will wake the whole world with your shrill voice," Said Ada as she stepped into the room. "Oh dear, this is much more serious than we were led to believe. Is she dead? It certainly, looks like it. Hello Gordon, it is nice to see you under whatever the circumstances. It is so reassuring to know you are on hand to deal with this sad situation."

Helen flushed as she had come to another conclusion to Gordon's presence. She took a closer look at Charlotte. Her blood matted hair was the only evidence that she wasn't merely taking a nap. She should have realised something wasn't right when she saw Charlotte was fully clothed and laid on top of the covers.

She blamed Gordon's presence. To see him here brought all sorts of emotions to the surface. Helen couldn't look at Gordon without seeing David alongside him. All those years at school Gordon had been the trusty sidekick to David the daredevil.

Helen had to take a few deep breaths to control her feelings. A quick glance at the waxen face of Charlotte focused Helen's mind and she took in the strange outfit and the bright blue shoes. When things like this happened she liked to organise. The only time she had ever fought with David was when she had ordered him around when she was near panicking. He hadn't appreciated her reaction.

She smoothed her hands down her skirt and said, "Gordon, take the poor girl's shoes off. She looks horribly uncomfortable. Have you taken a photo for your files and made notes? No? Well, let me run downstairs and get my own camera. It's much better than your point and shoot thingy. Get your notebook out and we can do the examination thoroughly. When do you expect the doctor to come?"

Helen's mind was a whirlpool of thoughts. She had been looking forward to this holiday and now poor Charlotte's death had changed all her plans. She wished she could have come a day later but pushed aside that thought. She owed Charlotte. Not because she was to blame but because they had a shared past. A shared pain.

Helen glanced over to Ada. Would her mother want to pack up and leave? She was pleased to see instead of running for home and safety, Ada seemed to be enjoying this new twist as she was peering closer at Charlotte's still form.

Helen sighed thankfully. Gordon looked tired slouched in the chair by Charlotte's bed. She couldn't leave him to do this alone. He has been a friend when she had needed one. She would leave him to face this alone either.

Footsteps on the stairs announced the arrival of Doctor McTierney from Ixopo. Helen said, "Come mother we should go so the doctor can have a proper look at poor Charlotte."

Ada followed her out. "I'll just pop over to our rooms for the camera." A smile touched Helen's lips. It seemed her mother was amiable to a little sleuthing for Charlotte's sake as well.

Helen stayed on the top landing looking around. No scrapes on the staircase. No scuff marks at all. Maybe it was the lower staircase Charlotte had fallen down? On this higher floor there was no offending mat to trip anyone up. Helen looked at the ceiling and saw a splatter of rusty marks on the roof. Perhaps an over-enthusiastic shake of a bottle.

But what liquid would be a rusty red colour? Ketchup? Originally developed to help with gastric problems, ketchup had never been very effective in its original form but was something the troops had brought home with them as a flavouring for food. The awful American sauce as her mother called it. Were there any Americans in residence?

Chapter Six

Helen just shook her head in confusion at the strange splatters on the ceiling as she listened with half an ear to the rumble from inside the room as the doctor made his examination. She couldn't quite hear the conversation, but a few words filtered through. After a quick glance to make sure no one was watching, Helen pressed her ear against the door.

"Blunt force trauma.... weapon .... Rigor mortis well set …" Oh, she thought, this doesn't sound at all like an accident. Ada joined her and, in a whisper, Helen told her what she had heard.

"Poor Gordon, he might need a little bit of help," Ada suggested. Helen's thoughts exactly.

Helen then looked up at the ceiling and pointed it out to Ada. "Could it be blood? Are we contaminating the scene of the crime, Mom?" Ada's husband and Helen's father had been a police surgeon for many years and they were well versed in what was acceptable, and what was not, at a crime scene.

Too late now to worry about destroying evidence. Whatever signs there might have been had been obscured by successive people walking through the area. The van Rooyen family and some of the construction workers from the jail project lived on this floor. And it didn't even take into account hotel staff busy with their daily tasks.

Helen motioned for her mother to hand over the camera and pointed it at the ceiling to take a considered shot of the splatter. She closed the leather flap over the lens and looped the strap around her wrist.

The bedroom door opened and Dr McTierney stepped out. "Good day ladies. I suppose you are waiting to dress the poor lady for her burial? Well, you'll have to wait. I have finished my examination and will go downstairs to write my report for the police. We will forgo an autopsy for now. The reason for the death is plain to see and I have no facility to do much more here in the hotel. Constable Brown, if you could be in charge of the body until the undertaker arrives. I will wait for the corpse to reach Ixopo before I do the autopsy."

He slipped off his gloves and carefully placed them into a paper bag. Rolling up the top he slipped it into his leather bag. He tucked the bag against his side as he strode down the stairs.

Gordon was desperately scribbling in his notebook when they returned to Charlotte's room. Trying to remember everything the doctor had said before he forgot anything vital or important most likely. Helen looked over his shoulder and said, "Gordon, you'll never be able to decipher this handwriting once you get back to the office. Give it here and let me write while you dictate."

Gordon hesitated for a moment before he offered the pencil and the notepad. He sat back in the chair with his eyes closed as he dictated. Helen smiled at him as she always felt comfortable around Gordon. It was most likely why she had sought him out when she had found out about David.

"Death consistent with a blunt force trauma to the base of the skull with a heavy object. Not possible to have been caused by a fall down the stairs due to accidental mishap. Time of death consistent with the time given by Miss Susanna van der Merwe as midnight on April 6th 1946. Victim is wearing a …? Helen what would you call her outfit?" Gordon asked.

"A floral blouse, bright blue skirt, just below the knee, and a pair of blue high heels with floral embellishment, heel of one shoe snapped. Three beaded bracelets, a bright multi-coloured necklace of beads and earrings to match. One earring missing." Helen reeled off the list of clothing as she wrote it down on the notepad for Gordon.

She looked up to see Ada carefully lifting the hair away from Charlotte's head. "Nasty cut on the side of the head just behind the ear. Mm, and I would say this gash on the back is the fatal blow. I can see brain tissue and bone amongst the blood." Ada motioned for the camera and Helen unwrapped the strap from her wrist. Ada took photos while Gordon confirmed Ada's findings with the doctor's words.

Helen glanced up from her notes when she heard Gordon falter in his retelling.

"Oh Gordon, you look like you are about to faint. You have gone all pale. Mom, see if you can get him a nice cup of tea sent up." Helen pushed Gordon's head down on his knees and waited for him to perk up a little bit.

"Sorry, I've been up all night and I think I might need a good bite to eat to get me back up and at it," Gordon mumbled from between his knees.

Ada arrived at her usual half-gallop with Delphinia and a tray of cake and tea balanced precariously, slopping milk over the side of the small milk jug.

"Gordon be a good man and eat this all up at once." Helen insisted. Gordon smiled. A much better response than she was used to from men when she got into a state and started ordering people around. She tapped the pencil on the open notebook nervously. Usually when she got like this people got angry with her. David mostly put up with it but Gordon had always been somewhat amused by her coping mechanism.

"All right, just as soon as I cover poor Charlotte up with a sheet or something. I have a huge aversion to eating in the presence of the dead. I shouldn't really after my time in the war, but it's something I just can't shake." When he tried to get up Helen hissed at him and covered Charlotte up with a clean sheet herself. She helped him to his feet and outside the room to where a couple of chairs overlooked the stairwell.

Gordon plonked himself down and waited to be served.

Helen watched the colour return to his cheeks as he ate. Even when he had finished most of the food she poured him another cup of milky sweet tea as soon as he'd finished his first.

Delphinia had retreated to the lower floors and no doubt would be telling her fellow staff members what she had seen. It wasn't every day that a woman died and a guest bossed around the policeman sent to investigate.

"My Gran would drink tea like this," Gordon said. "One cup of tea after another. Her teeth were brown as berries and Dad always said it was the Tannin in the tea staining them, but she didn't seem to care. She said tea was the great healer of all things bad."

Helen nodded to agree with him. She had known his grandmother and her proclivity for tea at any time of day or night. Some kind person had even put a cup and saucer on the top of her grave at her funeral. Not filled with tea, but rather with a posy of tiny violets.

"Oh, I remember your Gran so well. She said she wanted to lose weight and she hardly ate a thing. She said she had no idea why she was still so fat. But you and I laughed because we knew each time she had a cup of tea, she insisted on a biscuit or a scone to accompany it."

Once he had finished the second cup Helen pointed out the splatter on the ceiling and he stood on the chair to get a closer look while Ada placed the denuded tray onto a handy hall table out of the way.

"Mm, you could be right, Helen. But without the help, I have no idea how to prove it. We will just have to find other ways of solving the murder." Gordon put his hand out for the camera and Helen handed it up to him so he could take a photo of the evidence. She didn't tell him she had already taken photos. He was closer and more likely to take clearer shots.

"Okay, Gordon, let's have another look at the victim and see what else we can uncover," Helen said and they all looked at Charlotte once more for a closer examination. From top to toe they noted each and every little injury. Helen drew a crude outline of a person in the notebook and Ada used her comb to move the hair away from the injuries.

By the time they were finished it was two hours later and they all needed a break.

The film in the camera was used up, removed and replaced with a fresh one. Ada looked wilted. The notebook was full of Helen's neat handwriting and Gordon claimed it and stored it in his pocket.

"Time for lunch everyone. Not much else we can do here," announced Helen as she heard the faint call of the lunch bell.

CHAPTER SEVEN

Charlotte's bedroom door was locked and the key carefully placed in the inside pocket of Gordon's uniform as he escorted the two women downstairs. As they walked slowly down the stairs, he scrutinized the bannister. No marks denoted a desperately grasping hand, no scuff to show a shoe had scraped the stairs on their way down. The stairs looked as pristine as if they had been installed yesterday.

The missing earring was discovered while Helen had cleaned up for lunch. Hidden in the shadows of the skirting board just outside the bedroom door and had been duly noted and carefully stored in a paper-bag. One of many bags Gordon had brought with him from the city on the off-chance they might be needed.

Pamela Meaker was behind the counter at reception and waved to them gaily. "Seems like I am perfect for the job of receptionist. Mr. van Rooyen says he might hire me." Her face fell. Gordon was used to the swing of emotion around people after a death.

The guilt at even briefly being happy for some else's demise.

He patted her hand as Pamela's lips quivered. "Oh, how awful of me to take joy in Charlotte's accident."

Mr. van Rooyen came out of his office standing behind Pamela. "Shh, dear. We don't want to spook the guests."

Gordon nodded to the Mr. van Rooyen. Gordon would have to question people but it was better not to spook the killer beforehand. Mr. van Rooyen eyed Helen standing by Gordon.

Gordon cleared his throat. "Helen is a longtime friend."

Ada snorted. "Their whole silly lives. Best friends to Helen's poor David."

Gordon glanced at Helen to make sure the mention of David wasn't causing her any pain. There was a little hurt in her eyes but she wasn't about to break down.

Gordon said, "Helen and Ada will keep it quiet." The death would not stay a secret for long, but they were in agreement it would not be good for business, either for the police or the hotel to announce it before he could do some snooping.

Some of the workers from the jail project might decide to camp out at the site and Sue might find lodging over the highway, but the rest of the guests would just up and go home.

Not a prospect Mr. van Rooyen would enjoy. An empty hotel did not look good on the books. Gordon on the other hand, wanted to keep the details under wraps, firstly to make sure the killer didn't disappear as there was a good chance the killer was a guest, secondly the killer might accidently reveal something only he and Gordon knew.

Gordon took a seat in the dining room. Two women sat at a window seat on a two-person table and Helen waved to them as she took a seat at his table.

She nervously chatted with him. "Not many of the construction workers from the jail project came back for their midday meal. They probably prefer to eat close to their work."

Ada muttered to herself as she studied the menu up close.

She wasn't the only one avidly focused on feeding themselves. Steve sat with a pile of papers in front of him, deep in thought and absentmindedly shovelling in his food.

"I wonder where Maisie and the major are." Helen speculated.

Ada said, "They are old. They probably are taking a nap."

Gordon didn't want to point out to Ada that description also described her. Instead of wading into that conversation he studied the menu himself. He ordered a large serving of roast beef and vegetables with extra roast potatoes and pumpkin.

No one spoke until after the main course had been consumed. Gordon looked at his companions and thought if there had not been a murder, this would be a great way to spend a lunchtime.

He took out his notebook and pencil and leaned in close to his compatriots as he spoke softly.

"You know a few of the hotel guests, did you observe anything unusual? Some aggression towards Charlotte? And what on earth is her full name? Miss van der Merwe never mentioned a surname and Mr. van Rooyen hardly said a word to me when I arrived."

Gordon opened the notebook to a clean page. "I need to interview everyone in the hotel. I suppose I should have asked Mr. van Rooyen what her full name was." He looked around the almost empty dining room.

Helen folded the napkin and laid it next to her plate. "Hold on Gordon, I will see what I can find out from Ruth and Fiona. Did I tell you I went to school with Charlotte at St Cuthberts? No? Well, I have no idea what her surname was, always just knew her as Lottie. Let me talk to the sisters and see what they know."

Helen launched herself out of her seat and towards the two sisters. Gordon almost knocked over his chair to follow after her.

He'd just stepped up beside her as she launched into her questioning of the two young women. "Have you heard poor Charlotte had an accident? We were just wondering who knew her the best. Does she have a boyfriend or a special friend at all?"

Gordon peered down into two bright blue eyes that twinkled up at him with interest. Fiona was so used to men's admiration that it was second nature for her to flirt with any good-looking man around. She flicked her blonde hair off her forehead and crossed her very shapely legs as she leaned slightly forward.

Fiona then looked up at Helen and said, "Yes, she has a boyfriend. No idea who he is. Charlotte would get dressed up to the nines two or three times a week and take off for a walk. We'd tease her about it quite a bit of course. She never mentions who it is, but we have a suspicion he might be married because she doesn't seem to want to introduce him to the rest of us love starved ladies."

Ruth was the polar opposite to her sister and adjusted her skirt to cover her knees as she frowned slightly. Her brown hair was severely pulled back into a bun and her gray eyes were serious. Gordon noticed that her figure was much more feminine and rounded compared to her more streamlined sister. He thought she would look very pretty with her hair down and a smile on her face.

"Oh Fi, don't be mean. How do you know he's married? She might be keeping him a secret because she is scared we will snaffle him away from her. After her walks, she always dances in the gardens like a whirling dervish. She does have the most amazing ability to float on those ridiculous heels of hers like a dream. As to her surname? Steve, do you know Charlotte's surname?" Ruth called over the empty tables.

Steve lifted his head and shook it slightly as if to wake himself up. "Cooper. Her surname is Cooper. Her family is from somewhere on the coast. She was brought up by a maiden aunt I think. But the aunt died last month. Remember, she went away for a few days to attend the funeral and sort out the estate."

"Oh, now I remember," said Ruth. "Tongaat half an hour north of Durban. Beautiful spot with rock pools and wild bush right on the coast. Not really my cup of tea. I like mountains. Charlotte did say she attended a small country school when she was young and then went to some fancy boarding school for a few years."

Ruth opened a file from her pile of school books and pulled out a postcard. Holding it out to Gordon to look at, she said, "She sent me this while she was away. It's a picture of a rock pool that Charlotte thought I might enjoy. I love nature and I would love to go visit her there sometime. Maybe when I get a holiday from Mathilda?" Her whole face softened as she spoke of her student.

"The aunt had a small house overlooking the sea. Idyllic I suppose some might call it. Charlotte worked for a while at a hotel in Durban, but she said there was no future for her there after the war broke out. She spoke about dance competitions in the city hall. I think she was quite good at dancing. Not much dancing here in the mountains, but maybe now the men are back from the war things might get back to normal? Why don't you speak to Charlotte herself? Surely she could tell you all this information?"

Gordon went still. He wasn't ready to answer that question himself. So he bowed his head over his notes and made sure he got down all the details. Helen saved him with a flick of her wrist dismissing Ruth's questions. "Thanks Ruth. Yes, I could ask Charlotte of course, but she is not able to answer at the moment and I thought you girls might know. I went to school with Charlotte many years ago and I feel a bit silly not knowing the basics about her. And you Fiona, anything to add?" Helen smiled as she made her query.

"Aren't you the nosy parker, Miss Bell? Well, no, I don't have much in common with Charlotte. And I hate hospital rooms, so don't ask me to visit the poor girl. She seems nice enough, but much too flighty for me. I like someone who can hold down a conversation on general knowledge and not just the best place to buy a pair of shoes." Fiona smiled slightly to ameliorate her harsh words.

"Fi, behave yourself. Charlotte is a lovely girl. And yes, you do so like to know where to buy fancy shoes. It's just your agreement with the chocolate people, the McCarthy family, said you were not to spend too much time in the city otherwise you would be there every day if you could." Ruth looked so much like the schoolteacher she was, while she remonstrated with her sister, and Gordon had to hold in a smile as she observed the sibling interaction.

After lunch Gordon went to read through his notes and interview the other guests.

Chapter Eight

Helen decided to take a ride through town on her bicycle to clear her head and work off the second helping of chocolate pudding she had consumed. She went upstairs to change into more suitable clothing for doing exercise.

Wisp was curled up and sleeping in the sun on the window sill. Helen picked her up and said, "It's about time you got some sunshine outside, you lazy thing."

Where would a woman go to meet a man while dressed in high heels and a revealing outfit? Not too far. Those shoes were not meant for walking any distance at all.

She hadn't told Gordon she planned to do her own investigation. He'd most likely tell her not to bother.

Helen placed Wisp in the basket in front of her bike as she walked it down the drive. The drive was smooth enough for a car or a bicycle, but high heels were another thing entirely. One wrong step in the dark and you would have a very sore ankle.

Turning right at the T-junction, Helen pedaled slowly looking for clues. Wisp sat with her front paws on the edge of the basket pleased with her lot in life and the breeze in her fur.

The road dipped into a shallow stream and the ford was easy to navigate. But would a woman be prepared to get her shoes wet? Surely not. The air was heavy with bird song and the insidious creak of cicadas. Sunbeams played across the road and the breeze teased the tops of the trees creating movable patterns with the shadows of leaves.

Helen turned her bike around and pedaled back up the hill. A flash of something shiny in the bush caught her eye and she stopped. Climbing off the bike, she leaned it against a tree and went to investigate. Wisp joined her sniffing at the side of the road for a moment.

A path had been worn into the centre of a small glade. Orchids hung in the branches above Helen's head and bright daisies were sprinkled amongst the undergrowth.

A crude bower had been created by dint of placing a few pieces of corrugated iron between two trees. A handful of nails had been utilized to keep the iron in place. On the ground underneath the simple roof, was a sheet of board and a few cushions.

Helen peered through the undergrowth. To most people it might have suggested a place of refuge for a homeless person, but Helen spotted something indicating it was more likely a meeting place for lovers.

Two champagne glasses. A closer inspection, conducted by grabbing onto a handy branch and standing on tippy toes as Helen teetered precariously at the edges of the glade, uncovered a few empty bottles and a soft rug hidden behind a tree.

Wisp came closer to knead the blanket and Helen picked her up with a gentle rebuke. "No Wisp, this is not a place to sleep, especially for lazy cats. It could be important to Gordon. Now let's go."

Helen tickled Wisp behind her ear as she stood for a moment taking in the scene.

Careful not to disturb the site too much, Helen climbed back on her bike and went in search of Gordon and her mother. Wisp sat up in the basket as she observed the countryside around her with its new smells and senses.

CHAPTER NINE

Helen whistled softly as she entered the reception area. Ada sat speaking to Maisie and Gordon was nowhere to be seen. She heard gruff male voices emanating from behind a closed door and surmised it must be the office of the hotel manager.

Plonking herself down next to her mother, and keeping Wisp under control on her lap, Helen had to be satisfied with a lukewarm cup of tea and a cheese scone with lashings of rich golden butter as she waited. So much for working off the excesses of lunch, now she would have to do something to combat the scone, she thought as she took another bite.

Ada spoke to Maisie about Charlotte and her high heels. "She must buy those shoes of hers in the city. I doubt there would be a shop so far out in the country selling them. Not something farmers would wear."

"Oh yes, there is. A cute boutique in Underberg, not too far from here, they supply some top of the line clothing. You have to pay a little bit more than the prices in Pietermaritzburg or Durban, but not too expensive if it is what you like? I wouldn't imagine you are interested in extravagant clothing, dear Ada. You look like a woman of class and distinction. And you too Helen. A real lady and not like some of these youngsters who flaunt their bodies in such a scandalous way," Maisie griped.

Mr. van Rooyen and Gordon came out of the office with grim looks on their faces. Mr. van Rooyen called Pamela in from her post at the reception desk and then waited till everyone in the room was looking at him.

"Ahem, I have an announcement to make. Charlotte Cooper has died as a result of a vicious attack here in the hotel. I will tell the rest of the guests at dinner tonight, but until then, just know we are doing all we can to uncover the culprit and bring them to justice. We understand a few of you might feel the need to leave under these circumstances, but we urge you to first see Constable Brown and he will take your details for further reference."

Helen asked Ada, "Do you want to leave?"

Ada looked smug over her cup of tea. "Of course not, dear. We can't leave poor old Gordon to sort this out on his own. Way too exciting by far to leave."

Helen almost forgot she had some exciting discoveries to share with Ada and Gordon as she watched Maisie go a strange grey colour and keel over in her seat.

Maisie slipped right off the chair and landed in a puddle of beige silk on the maroon carpet which had been the scene of Wisp's preening the day before.

Ada jumped into action and quickly had any sensitive areas covered and swung Maisie round until her feet rested on the chair and her head on the carpet. Helen recognised her mother's nursing façade.

Her mother looked up at her and without asking Helen ran off to find a wet cloth as Maisie started making gurgling noises. Wisp tucked firmly under her arm Helen ignored her feline's complaints.

By the time she returned Maisie had her eyes open but was still a strange colour. Ada grabbed the cloth from Helen and proceeded to wipe the patient's face and neck. Gagging sounds had Helen rushing off to find a bucket in case Maisie decided to regurgitate her tea and scones.

Delphinia came to help and they soon had the lady lying on the couch with cushions propping up her feet and a soft rug over her lap.

Helen patted her hand kindly. "Just stay there a moment, Maisie. You'll be fine. It was just the shock of the terrible news about Charlotte. Shame on you Mr. van Rooyen for being so abrupt. Some ladies are sensitive about things like death."

Helen glowered at Mr. van Rooyen as he stood shame-faced at the foot of the couch. He should have been a little more tactful in announcing poor Charlotte's demise. Though Helen wasn't sure what words would have worked. The letter from David's commanding officer had been kind and yet they had destroyed her world.

"Yammer, yammer Mevrou." He apologised in Afrikaans before going off. Gordon followed after Mr. van Rooyen to observe the reaction of the staff while. Helen glanced at her mother but it seemed she had Maisie in hand. She followed after Gordon. Wisp was not pleased to be restrained for so long and Helen allowed her cat its freedom for the moment.

Helen followed Gordon and Mr. van Rooyen to the staffroom. His entrance brought silence to the room and the staff who lounged around. Mr. van Rooyen looked around and asked, "I've got bad news. Charlotte died last night. The Constable here would like to speak with all of you. If anyone knew if Charlotte had any family or friends and might have an interest in Charlotte's demise please tell me. Her records don't have her next of kin. So we don't know who will take on the funeral or put her to rest."

Helen said, "I went to school with Charlotte, but I have no idea if she had any family around." She turned to Mr. van Rooyen and said, "If you would like, I can help with the arrangements. I have done this before. My Dad was a surgeon and we were often involved in the final moments of people's lives. It will be no trouble Mr. van Rooyen and I am sure Constable Brown can assure you we are good people." She glanced at Gordon and he nodded in agreement.

"Ya, Miss Bell. It would be acceptable and much appreciated. As long as it will not ruin your holiday to do this final service for your school friend and our work colleague. I will even give you a refund on your room. Baie dankie." Mr. van Rooyen thanked her in Afrikaans. He looked overly relieved. She wasn't sure if she approved of his lack of responsibility to one of his employees but at least Charlotte would be laid to rest.

Chapter Ten

It was almost three in the afternoon before Ada, Gordon and Helen could take a walk and inspect the love bower.

"Just show me the place you found Helen and then keep out of the way and let me do what I am trained to do," Gordon announced. He had been pleased with their help in the early morning but now his masculine pride and responsibilities as a policeman had re-asserted themselves.

He squared his shoulders firmly in his khaki uniform and took a deep breath as he stood up straighter.

Ada had a sturdy walking stick with her and Helen had her cat on a leash in a vain attempt at stopping Wisp from uprooting some of the more delicate plants. The cat had a penchant for ripping newly planted flowers and dragging them into the house.

Helen didn't bother to even acknowledge him and instead stalked off. Ada hummed to herself. "You better get moving, boy. She will leave you behind."

He took off across the bowling lawn, through the rose gardens and down the bank onto the road. Helen was slowed down, allowing him to catch up, by Wisp doing her best to make the short trip as difficult as she could, sitting down to lick herself at every opportunity.

Helen brought them to the path she had found in her earlier travels. Gordon noted there were distinct footprints on the path and it would need to be examined further. He wondered if there was a packet of plaster of Paris in the town to make moulds of the indentations. The bower was just as Helen had left it, except to note the rug and the glasses had vanished.

"Gordon, I promise you there were glasses and a blanket here earlier." Helen tutted obviously frustrated at the destruction of her discovery, which led him to believe she really had seen the rug and the glasses. Ada used her walking stick to poke around, but nothing new was discovered.

Gordon glared at Ada and said, "Mrs. Bell, if you could refrain from disturbing the site. I would appreciate it."

"No problem at all, my boy. I just thought I would give you a helping hand," Ada said sweetly.

"They were here. Someone must have come and cleaned up so we would think it was a homeless shelter," Helen said. Running her fingers through her hair. He watched her fingers and wondered if her hair was soft and silky as it looked. He frowned at his own thoughts and shook himself.

Gordon studied the ground and found another set of footprints. Firstly, the indentations of a pair of high heeled shoes and secondly, a boot footprint. Nothing unusual in its markings or size. Average is what would best describe it and Gordon took out a measuring tape to make sure of his visual estimation.

As he bent closer, he noted a small nick in the heel. If, or when, they found the culprit, they would be able to identify the shoe print. He was not convinced this had anything to do with the murder, but all avenues needed to be covered.

He sighed as he looked around. "Helen, thanks for finding this lovers' shack but I really don't think it has much to do with the murder. I will make a thorough examination in case it has any bearing."

Helen took photos of the interior of the love shack and then stood back a few steps to take another look around. Gordon put his hand out for the camera and did his own series of snaps to capture all aspects of this love-nest.

He was not in the least disturbed when the women moved away slightly. In fact, he preferred it, as he was able to concentrate without the distraction of Helen and her perfume.

CHAPTER ELEVEN

Wisp found an interesting smell and pulled at the strap in Helen's hand as she meowed softly.

"Okay Wisp, we can attend to your business now. We are all finished up here. Why can't you be normal and use a flower bed like other cats do?" Helen scolded her cat in a distracted manner.

Wisp pulled a little more and Helen allowed her the leeway. The cat made a strange noise usually reserved for encouraging birds to come closer. Not because it ever actually worked, but it was very distinctive. Helen sighed and went to see the treasure Wisp was wanting her to examine. She bent down and peered under the bush expecting to see a cowering field mouse or at worst, a snake.

"Oh, clever girl. Mom, Gordon come look what Wisp has found for us." Helen picked a corner of a piece of card, carefully by an edge to reveal a photograph. Shaking errant leaves and dirt from its surface they could see a smiling Charlotte looking out at them.

A male stood next to her, but his features were badly marred by the dirt. "I will need to take this back to my room and see what I can unearth." Gordon barely smiled at his own the pun. He dropped to his knees next to Helen and she stepped back surprised by the warmth that flittered over her skin having him so close.

He ran his hands through the grass and dirt to see if he could find anything more in the spot the cat had found. A stained envelope from a photographic laboratory in Johannesburg was pulled from the leaf mould. She leaned over him to see if she could make out the full address on the envelope but Gordon had it tucked away in a clean handkerchief and gently placed in his uniform pocket.

"Helen it would be more appropriate if I took the photograph back to Pietermaritzburg. You have to let me do my job and stop trying to be the investigator. Really I can do this on my own you know." Gordon wiped the leaves and mud off his trousers as he said this.

Emotion warred inside her. She hadn't had time to examine her reaction to him but she knew being close to him while he investigated would make it more pronounced. That outcome though was what confused her. Did she want to have any kind of reaction to Gordon? Gordon who had been her friend for so many years. All of that didn't change that she felt like she owed something to Charlotte. Maybe it was guilt that she barely remembered her. Or that she hadn't been her friend while they had been at school.

"Oh no, Gordon. I would never want to take over the investigation. You are the policeman after all. Can I try to remove some of the surface dirt? We can't wait for the police headquarters to clean it up if there is a chance of catching the killer. I promise not to do any damage. I will be very careful and if I think evidence is going to be lost, I will stop immediately," Helen pleaded. She couldn't be pushed off this investigation though she wasn't going to examine her motives any longer.

Gordon pursed his lips as he thought it over. His hand briefly going to the pocket where the envelope and photo resided.

"Okay Helen, you can keep the photo for a few hours. I am trusting you not to let me down. If it will speed up this murder case, then give it a try. But be very careful. I beg you. I am not sure this has anything to do with Charlotte's murder, so I will give you a little leeway with the photo."

Leaning down so Gordon could not see her satisfied smile, Helen tickled Wisp under her chin and promised her all sorts of treats as a result of her clever fossicking. All three humans and a very pleased cat, sauntered back across the lawns. Helen could barely contain her excitement at the thought of uncovering the identity Charlotte's boyfriend.

Chapter Twelve

Gordon opened the door for her and her mother.

As they entered the reception Helen spotted Musa and two other males navigating the stairs with a large wooden box which was presumably their home-made coffin for Charlotte.

"Wait Musa," called Helen "Let's see if we can find a nice sheet or bed cover to line the coffin. Musa, don't put Miss Charlotte in it until I can do something about a lining." Musa smiled and nodded. The men put the coffin down and all hunkered down on their haunches in the time honoured way of Zulu men since time immemorial.

The reception area transformed into a semblance of an undertaker's waiting room as they patiently waited for the women to create the rightful and respectful resting place for their colleague.

"Pamela, Pamela?" Helen called to the empty reception desk. Instead of Pamela, Delphinia came out of the dining room and informed them, "Madam Pamela was busy elsewhere but I can help."

When she was apprised of the need for a nice sheet for the coffin, she quickly went into the cupboard under the stairs and came out with an embroidered cloth.

"Oh, perfect Delphinia. Miss Charlotte will be happy to spend eternity lying on such a beautiful piece of material."

Delphinia crouched down to tuck in one side of the embroidered cloth into the now open coffin. "It belongs to Miss Charlotte. She bought it last month when she went to Underberg. She said it was for when she would marry one day soon and she was going to make a pretty skirt with it."

Delphinia suddenly looked sad at the thought Charlotte would never fulfil her wish to be a blushing bride. Helen could relate. She had her own chest of linens she had collected for her own day that had yet to see any use.

"Miss Charlotte has been teaching me proper English. She was a very kind lady." Tears streamed from her eyes, Delphinia finished smoothing the cloth down and hurried away.

Ada held Wisp while Helen and Gordon finished folding the material into a base of the coffin. Musa, Simeon and Sipho stood with heads bowed as this was done and then lifted the casket to their shoulders and ascended the stairs. The men softly sang a dirge to a fallen colleague in Zulu as they performed this service. Their deep baritone voices evoking feelings of sadness as they slowly marched up the stairs towards Charlotte.

Gordon and Ada went to Charlotte's room to ensure she was placed in the coffin in a respectful manner while Helen took Wisp back to her bedroom.

Pulling the lamp closer and finding a soft cloth to wipe the photograph took but a moment. Helen found the dirt difficult to dislodge and she resorted to dipping the cloth into a glass of water and gently working at the edge of the stain. She looked over her shoulder to be sure Gordon had not entered the room and was observing her.

She had promised to do the minimum of work to uncover the other person in the photo and if Gordon could see her now, he might not think it was the minimum. Bit by bit the man was revealed. The face remained stubbornly covered by a blotch of decomposing leaves and Helen was scared to scrub too harshly in case she destroyed the features completely.

Dipping the cloth in the water and then wringing it out, she smoothed it over the photograph so it was gently pressing down on the offending dirt. Turning to Wisp, she said, "Nothing much I can do until this lot softens. I promised Gordon I would not destroy any evidence. Let's hope I can still look him in the eye after this little trick."

Helen stood at the window for a moment when she noticed Wisp was resolutely looking at a spot not far from the bed. "Wisp, what is wrong with you? Come here daft cat."

As Helen bent down to pick up the cat she felt a cold cloud envelop her. Her hair stood on end and she couldn't help but shiver. Helen's grandmother had the ability to see ghosts, but she herself didn't have the gift. Instead she had a talent manifested through dreams. A short nap could reveal the most amazing insights into all sorts of phenomenon and secrets. Many was the time Helen had known the answer to strange occurrences after a snooze in a cozy chair. Nieces and nephews all stood in awe of their Auntie Helen and her all Seeing Eye.

Looking at Wisp, she said, "Okay my girl, time for us to have a lie down." She put a 'Do Not Disturb' sign on the door, removed her shoes and got comfortable. Wisp was happy to join her mistress on the bed, but she kept a wary eye on the spot at the foot of the bed which had fascinated her earlier.

Helen had barely closed her eyes when a state of dreaming overcame her as she dropped off into sleep.

A radiant Charlotte appeared in front of her. She held the photograph to her chest and smiled happily looking straight at Helen. "I knew we would be real friends the moment I saw you all those years ago. I want to introduce you to someone special," She said holding out the photograph so Helen could see it clearly.

"We were going to get married. He wanted to tell his wife about us next week. He isn't the one who hurt me. He loves me. He *loves* me." She started to fade as she danced around the room on her high heels and Helen could feel her slipping away to another realm and she knew the nap was almost over.

As she battled her way through the fog around her, she saw other personages. A sad man sitting in a burning building with his hand held out as if looking for help. Zulu warriors stood with assegais dripping in blood. Two men dressed in construction clothing of a bygone era and even a little dog watched her as she drifted past them in her sleep.

They all looked sad and lost and Helen wanted to help them in any way she could. But maybe not today. Today was about Charlotte.

The mists of sleep cleared and she could feel the air around her change and crackle back into life. Barely moments had passed since she had returned to her room and she felt energised with excitement at this new discovery.

Helen's eyes popped open and she went to where the photograph had been coved with the soft cloth. Easing it off, she was confronted with the same photograph she had seen held by Charlotte in her dream.

Charlotte and Steve? Steve? The happily married man who had spoken of his pride in his children and his wife in the city. Steve who seemed like the soul of honesty and trust. Steve the adulterer.

Helen sat back in the chair and Wisp jumped up to receive a cuddle. Helen wondered, not for the first time, if Wisp was the one who could really see ghosts and she was the gateway for Helen to receive the visitations during the dreams. But she knew it was not so.

Helen could not remember the first time she had dreamed of people who had died and even those still alive, but in a strange way not like a normal dream at all. It was when she was very young and she had woken up and asked if Uncle George would be there in time for lunch. Ada had said Uncle George was not expected to visit until the following week and where did Helen get such a strange idea. Uncle George had walked through the door at that moment to the surprise of Ada but not to Helen.

Granma had given Helen a strange look and smiled conspiratorially at this young girl with the prescience. Ada had thought Helen might have heard of her uncle's approach in some other way and thought no more of it. It was only as she grew up and had many more strange dreams that her family knew she was different.

No one mentioned her gift to outsiders. Much as they did not talk about Granma and her ability to chat to the deceased. They knew many people would find it odd and even weird.

Auntie Ruby, Ada's sister, did séances for money and Granma had always said it was sheer hokery pokery and was dangerous to all involved. Granma kept a close watch on Helen until the day her Granma had died. Her final words had been for Helen. "You have a great gift not many people understand. Guard it well my sweet for it can be a treasure and a help all through your life."

Gran had kissed Helen softly and then closed her eyes and joined the many loved ones who had proceeded her through the veil of death to a beautiful spirit world and many were waiting eagerly to welcome her into their embrace.

Helen remembered her Granma with affection. "I wish you were here Gran. I could use your help."

Chapter Thirteen

Helen found Gordon in one of the lounges. "Aren't you surprised?" she asked after informing him of the identity of the man in the photo.

Actually, Gordon was not surprised. He had seen too many trustworthy men do despicable things in the name of love. He had only been a policeman for a few months, but he knew love was a strange addiction and made people did many things they would normally never think of. Steve now became his prime suspect.

"Thanks Helen. This has certainly been an amazing help to me. Who would have thought that such goings on were being played out in this tiny backwater?" Gordon leaned forward and kissed Helen on her cheek.

"Gordon you are blushing. You know I would do anything for you. Well, anything to help find the offender anyway." Helen kissed Gordon on his cheek in return and then wiped off a smudge of pink lipstick. She wet her finger by licking it and gently erased the tell-tale mark. He was grateful as it would not do for people to see the policeman with signs of affection on his cheek.

Gordon was still blushing as he walked down the stairs and went in search of the hotel manager. He spoke to Mr. van Rooyen about Steve and was told he was a hard taskmaster but paid all his bills on time and was considered a fair boss by his workers. It was not long before the workmen from the jail started arriving after their work day had finished and headed straight for the pub.

Gordon found the sisters watching the men and drinking. He stopped to listen to their conversation before he revealed his presence.

Fiona looked over at the drinking men in the pub and said, "There are a few good-looking blokes there, but not much in the way of money. A pity, they could be quite good around the house with all those muscles. Johan is a hunk, but not husband material. He is bad news. A new girl each week hanging onto his every word. It never lasts long. I wouldn't mind Gert. Man that man has moves. But he doesn't look at any of the girls. I wonder if he prefers men." Tossing back a wine, she offered to have another round ordered.

Ruth said, "We need to have some lemonade so we don't get drunk Fi. And stop ogling those poor boys. You will just get into trouble, and not the type of trouble you love. I can't imagine you pregnant and living in a tent. Realistically those boys have not a penny to rub together and you would hate the life they can offer." She called over the waitress and ordered some lemonades. Toasting their afternoon with ice cold lemonade, they looked around the quaint little pub and its patio.

Fiona sighed deeply and turned to her sister. "Thanks Sis. I know I shouldn't get mixed up with those youngsters. But what a waste to have an excess of men and hardly any competition around. Sue isn't exactly keen and Charlotte is—was in love with love."

Gordon smiled at the two sister's view of the men. It had been one of his motivations to become a policeman to have enough to keep a wife. There were many men looking for work now that they had returned from the war. Unfortunately, it had meant he had to move further afield than he had intended.

He skirted the two women so they wouldn't know that he had been eavesdropping and went into the pub itself.

Gordon found the workers all in the pub having an ice-cold beer together. There was loud laughter as the men joked with each other and teased one another about the day's happenings.

"Johan today you will pay for the beers. It is the beers of shame for you matey. Leaving a hammer on the scaffolding could have given someone a serious headache. I think you were thinking of a pretty young lady and not on your job. Not good. Not good at all. Who else is a contender for the beers of shame? Sam? Not checking the electricity was switched off before you started working around the live wire. You could have been more than a bright spark, you could have been a dead bright spark. Yes, definitely beers of shame for you too mate."

Gordon noted a few sheepish grins from Steve's work mates. Though little remorse. This seemed like a ritual for the men. Most likely they had all done something stupid at one time or other. It was the nature of the work. Human error could cause life threatening injuries and this was one way of dealing with a reprimand.

Johan paid for the first round. As Helen was the only woman recently to have arrived at the hotel Gordon worried that Johan's latest lady love was Helen. He didn't like the way his chest tightened at the thought. He would talk to the man later but right then he needed to question Steve. Before he could find Steve Gert caught his arm. "Hey, Constable why don't you join us for a drink."

"I'm on duty. Sorry. I have to speak with Steve."

Gert waved his drink. "One won't hurt you. Besides he might be my boss but Steve is a jerk."

Gordon pulled out of the man's grasp and without another word went to find Gert's boss.

Steve sat at a table tucked near the stairs. Gordon approached and dropped his hand on the construction boss's shoulder, he leaned down and whispered in his ear. "Steve. Can I have a word in private with you?"

Steve flushed bright red and then got up without a word and followed Gordon out the pub and upstairs to Mr. van Rooyen's office.

Mr. van Rooyen stayed behind his desk and Gordon pulled two chairs so he was facing Steve. He indicated Steve should sit and then introduced himself, "I'm Constable Brown. Mr. van Rooyen can attest to that fact. I'm investigating the sad death of Charlotte Cooper." Not saying another word, he sat and looked at Steve.

Mr. van Rooyen started to say something after about two minutes, but Gordon held up his hand to silence him. Steve seemed to look everywhere except at Gordon. His hands were shaking and his lips trembled until finally he raised his eyes and said, "What do you want to know about Charlotte?"

Still not saying a word, Gordon smiled and waited. Silence could be the best interrogator, if used properly. Steve started to sob quietly in his chair and Mr. Van Rooyen made a move towards him, but again, Gordon stopped him. The questioning had progressed much as Gordon had hoped and from now on it should get interesting.

"I didn't mean to have an affair with the poor girl. She deserved better than me. But I'm far from home with lots of responsibilities and I needed a kind ear to hear my complaints. Charlotte was a listening ear and it developed from there into love. We didn't mean to fall in love. I didn't mean to do this. And now she is dead and it's all my fault."

Mr. van Rooyen handed Steve a large clean handkerchief and a glass of iced water.

"If I had only been honest with her, then she might not have tripped over the carpet and fallen down the stairs. She was coming to meet me at our special place." Looking accusingly at Mr. van Rooyen he said, "You should have nailed the carpet down. It was an accident waiting to happen. You are just as culpable as I am for her death."

Gordon had been taking notes and now looked up in surprise at this outburst. "She didn't die from falling down the stairs, Steve. The carpet was not at fault, or Mr. van Rooyen or even you."

Now it was Steve's turn to look surprised. "Yes, it was. All the guys heard it from the African staff. A fall down the stairs. Sue was there, wasn't she? Then how did Charlotte die if it wasn't from an accident? Not suicide? Please not. I couldn't live with myself if I thought she had killed herself over me." His pleading eyes looked at Gordon for relief and clarification.

"No, not suicide. But we will want to know if anyone can verify your whereabouts at midnight last night."

Steve nodded his head. "Ya, Sam, Gert and Johan and I were playing darts and I forgot all about meeting Charlotte. We went upstairs at eleven thirty and we were getting ready for bed when it must have all must have happened. We didn't hear a thing. I have been worried sick Charlotte was on her way to meet me and I had forgotten our date. But why do you want to know where I was and such like? It was an accident wasn't it?"

Not wanting to reveal too much, Gordon had no choice but to give Steve the minimum of information. "She was killed by someone in the hotel and then the offender pushed her down the stairs. We think by the time Miss Van der Merwe found her, Charlotte was already deceased."

Steve shook his head as he took in this new information. "You don't think I did it, do you? I'm a bit of a cad with women but I'd have never hurt them physically and especially not Charlotte. Why would I do that? She thought I was going to marry her and she was happy to do my bidding. Shucks man, I had it good. I would have been stupid to kill her. If I had wanted to get rid of her I had the perfect excuse. I'm married for goodness sake. All I had to do was tell her that my wife would not give me a divorce and play the victim until the next job came along. I have done it before. I leave them crying and believing that I wanted to marry them and loved them but my wife and children would not allow me to follow my heart."

Steve laughed softly. "The women always believed my stories. I don't need to be the evil man in their eyes, I leave that to my wife. By the way my long-suffering wife has threatened to divorce me many times but is a Catholic girl and believes in turning the other cheek."

Gordon and Mr. van Rooyen looked at each other and then at Steve in disgust. "Stay here, Steve. I'm going to call the other men up to corroborate your story. I'm sure you think what you did is just a game but I'm not convinced you didn't resort to violence. Who knows what a man like you is capable of? I'll be right back," Gordon said as he stood up.

Sam, Gert and Johan were called up from the pub to offer their alibis and collaborate that they were with each other in their large dormitory bedroom at the time of the crime. Each one said the same thing, they had gone up the stairs from the pub together and got ready for bed together. The only time they had not been together was when they had gone to the bathroom at different times.

Gordon carefully recorded each men's statements and had them each sign and date their own declaration.

CHAPTER FOURTEEN

The interviews were interrupted when the hearse arrived to remove Charlotte. Gordon excused the men as Mr. van Rooyen called all the staff to join him to farewell the dear departed work mate.

The staff lined the reception area and started ululating and crying in a way that had the guests all reaching for their own handkerchiefs. The female staff members threw their aprons over their faces and the men with their deep voices gave a base note to the ululations. Some of the guests could be seen wiping away a tear or two.

Gordon took up a position by the door and watched the others. Hoping he could see the guilt etched on the killer's face.

Steve saluted the coffin as it passed by and many of the ex-servicemen did the same. Charlotte had been well liked amongst the guests.

Maisie sobbed into her husband's shoulder affected more than the other women. Though that could be put down to her sensitive nature.

Sue stood wringing her hands and tried not to look at the coffin. Fiona and Ruth stood holding hands and Helen and Ada stepped back to allow Pamela to touch the lid of the wooden box. Pamela had a posy of flowers she had hastily picked from the garden and placed them gently on the lid.

Tears rolled down her cheeks as she walked down the line of mourners and offered them each a flower to place on the coffin.

Gordon followed Charlotte outside to the waiting vehicle. He made sure everything was secure and that Charlotte would get to the doctor and her autopsy.

The doors to the hearse we shut and the undertaker in his black coat tails and top hat solemnly bowed to the mourners. Climbing behind the wheel of his vehicle he nodded his head to Mr. van Rooyen and Gordon before engaging the gears.

They all stood in silence as the hearse started its slow journey. Sam and Steve started singing a hymn with many of the guests joining in the chorus.

"Abide with me; tis eventide. The day is past and gone; the shadows of the evening fall; the night is coming on. Within my heart a welcome guest, within my home abide. O Saviour, stay this night we me; Behold, tis eventide. O Saviour, stay this night with me; behold, tis eventide."

As the last notes echoed through the misty trees people hung their heads in silent contemplation. The hearse made its way down the driveway and into the darkening countryside.

The singing had brought more tears to the assemblage. Helen stopped at his elbow. He glanced back at her and noticed the tears on her cheek. He dug out the last of his handkerchiefs and handed it to her. She muttered a thank you before dabbing at her eyes.

Slowly the staff and then the guests turned and went about their activities. Helen asked, "What did you find out? From Steve, I mean."

He shook his head. She sighed and said, "Another dead end."

"She was meeting him but he isn't our killer."

CHAPTER FIFTEEN

Dinner was a sombre time. Gordon was reluctant to break the mood so he kept mostly to himself. Helen and her mother came to sit with him but they all ate their dinner in silence, as did many of the other guests.

After the meal Helen and Gordon sat outside and had a glass of juice each while Ada went to read in her room. The noise from the pub slowly increased as the evening wore on. Gordon could hear the sound of men toasting the life of Charlotte. He enjoyed the quiet moment with Helen. He asked, "You've been good?"

Helen frowned at him so he added, "I know it was hard when you found out about David. I was worried."

Her smile was just a little sad. "It hasn't been easy but—It will be alright."

He knew she was hiding something but it was clear she didn't want to share what was bothering her. He reached out and took her hand in his own.

Helen tightened her grip in his and guided him to the door of the pub to hear the stories.

Sam raised his glass and said, "To Charlotte. I remember the first time we met, she was giggling at a silly riddle. I asked her what it was all about and she said it was a riddle and if I could figure it out then she would give me a kiss. She said, 'what goes up a chimney down but does not come down a chimney up?' I didn't have a clue of course. But she told me the answer was an umbrella and then she said, 'you can kiss me on the cheek if you like.' What a kind woman she was." He bowed his head in sorrow.

Johan raised his glass and said, "To all the women we have loved. May they remember us with the fondness we feel for them and not remember all the bad things we have done."

Steve sat quietly while others around him spoke about Charlotte, until suddenly he stood up and said, "I drink to her high heels, her infectious laugh, and her sparkling eyes and to all the moments she gave to me brightening my life. To Charlotte, we will miss you."

Gert did not drink the toast offered by Steve but said, "To Charlotte who died too young. May we always remember the good times? I wish her happiness as she dances with the angels in Heaven."

The day finally came to its close with many of the guests drowning their sorrows at the pub. Mr. van Rooyen was happily counting out the cash from his bonanza evening at the pub when Gordon came in to tell him he had finished for the day and would continue questioning people in the morning.

Mr. van Rooyen nodded and added, "I'm putting a guard on the stairs for the safety of the guests. He is a trusted worker and I will give him instructions he is not to allow any strangers access to the bedrooms. Do you want me to do anything else for the security of the people here under the hotel roof?"

Gordon said, "We have no idea who did the deed yet. All leads seem to have come to a dead end. Tomorrow I'll interview the rest of the guests, with your permission of course. And then interview the staff. I like your idea of a night watchman, it will give the guests a sense of safety. Do you have somewhere

I could sleep for the night? I'm afraid it is too far to travel home and back again tomorrow."

"Sure. We have a room prepared for you. Sadly, not the best but it will do in a pinch." Mr. van Rooyen led the way through the hotel and outside down a path to a block of rooms Gordon had thought was staff quarters. The room was neat and tidy but very simple in its furnishings. A single bed, a desk and a chair almost filled the tiny room.

Unconcerned about the simplicity of the room. He had slept in worse places while in the war and at least there was no gunfire to keep him awake. He undressed and lay on the bed staring up at the ceiling. Tired as he was he could not get to sleep as his head grappled with all the things he had learned since arriving early in the morning.

Gordon smiled slightly as he thought of Helen and how efficient she had been. If it were not such a serious occasion, he would feel they were back at home trying to figure out a tricky solution to a conundrum.

Finally, he nodded off only to be plagued with strange dreams of blood splashed walls and eerie ghosts doing despicable things to people. He saw a house being burned to the ground as a man cried amongst the flames.

Zulu assegais appeared to be stabbing him and blood curdling screams had Gordon sitting up in his bed long before daybreak.

Sweat dripped down his face as his heart pounded in his chest. He could almost believe the demons of the night were still all around him as he hastily dressed and went in search of more peaceful surroundings. The room felt chill and unwelcoming and he was happy to search out somewhere more amenable.

Gordon found a comfy bench outside on the terrace and took out his trusty notebook only to be disturbed by an overly affection Wisp. She jumped up onto his lap and then rubbed her head against his chin. "You are right, old girl. I need to shave. No good showing myself looking like a hobo for your beautiful mistress."

"Beautiful, am I?" Helen bent down and kissed Gordon on his cheek as she sat in the chair next to him. "Wisp was insistent we come outside, and now I see why. I think the silly cat has a crush on you Gordon. She is usually very stand offish with people, but you she loves."

Gordon offered his arm to Helen and they took a slow stroll around the garden. Gordon picked a dew speckled rose for Helen and she laughed as she remembered this was the second morning in a row a handsome young man had offered her a floral tribute.

They saw Steve, Sam, Gert and Johan walk past on their way to work. Johan grabbed his heart with both hands and called out, "Oh be still my beating heart, for the fair maiden has chosen another suitor." The other men laughed and continued on their way through the mist shrouded valley.

"What was it all about Helen? An admirer? Am I stealing you away from your true love?" Gordon asked with a smile on his face but a lump in his heart.

"Are you jealous, Gordon? No, Johan and even Sam and Gert have been really good to me since we arrived and given me many undeserved compliments. Sweet boys, but I am not interested at all," Helen stated as she smiled up into Gordon's grey eyes. Her hand lay in his for a moment and the world stopped for a nanosecond. Helen sighed and pulled her hand away then went in pursuit of Wisp, who seemed intent on chasing a small butterfly.

"Time to go in and get washed up for the day. And you need a shave Gordon. I agree with Wisp, you are looking like a hobo who has slept rough under a bush." Helen laughingly led them all back inside the hotel.

Chapter Sixteen

At breakfast Gordon met Matilda and her mother, Mrs. van Rooyen. They must have arrived during the hubbub of yesterday's dramas. Matilda looked like a stiff breeze would knock her over and noticing her mother's haunted eyes was enough to know things were not well with the young girl.

Ruth sat with them and silently ate her breakfast while Matilda chatted on about their time in the city.

Matilda had no problem conversing between bites of toast. "The cars were everywhere. Mom had to run across the road dragging me behind her so we didn't get run over. It was fun. We ate at a café in the park and fed the swans. They were really beautiful. Have you seen swans Constable?"

Not waiting for an answer, she continued, "Mom said I could eat a big doughnut covered with chocolate and sprinkles looking like hearts. We visited lots of doctors and the hospital. They were not nice. The people were nice, but they kept pricking me with needles." She burbled on until her mother told her to eat up and stop talking.

Gordon enjoyed the innocent conversation and happily ate while young Matilda ignored her mother and continued her monologue of life in the city. "We stayed in a hotel, but not like this hotel. There was a radio in each room. And the bathrooms had showers as well as baths. Mom said I could have a bubble bath the one night and it smelled like perfume."

She jumped from one subject to another and her mother just shrugged in resignation as her precocious daughter regaled them with inconsequential facts and memories.

Mrs. van Rooyen waited for Matilda to slow down before she asked how Gordon had slept and he was loath to say the room was not a very pleasant. So, he lied and said he had a peaceful night's rest.

"Now isn't that interesting? We used to rent the room out for a pittance, but then the guests all complained about ghostly visits. Someone even said they had seen blood dripping from the walls. Nonsense of course. The hotel is quite new and we have never had anything terrible happen here until yesterday. I'm so glad you were not affected by the negative words of others." Mrs. van Rooyen delicately dabbed her mouth with her napkin, careful not to disturb her carefully applied make up.

Gordon was used to following a hunch. If Mrs. Van Rooyen implied that his dreams were a ghostly visitation he might see where it led. "Have there ever been any fires? Or Zulu warriors with assegais in the area?"

Mrs. van Rooyen looked at him closely before saying, "Yes, the original owner of the hotel went bankrupt and soon afterwards died in a house fire. But not here in the hotel of course. As to Zulu warriors. Well, there was a story about a battle fought near here. But again, not in the hotel. Quite a bloody battle as I recall. Many years ago, now. Long before the hotel was even a dream. Perhaps as much as one hundred years ago. The local tribes still talk of it and say it is thagkathi, witchcraft, and never to be spoken about."

She shivered slightly as she finished saying the word. "Time to go Matilda. Medicine first and then maybe a short lesson if you please Ruth. Goodbye Constable Brown. I do hope we can find a speedy resolution to this nasty business." She wafted out of the dining room on a cloud of perfume and talcum powder.

Ruth stayed seated and once her student and her mother had left, she leaned in and said to Gordon, "The dreadful room is notorious for strange happenings. No one ever sleeps there more than one night. You did well to get any sleep at all. Delphinia will tell you none of the African staff will even go inside to clean it. The receptionist is always assigned to change the sheets and sweep and dust the room. No idea what has caused it, but it must be something awful because even I won't go inside. I get to the door and my hair stands up on end. Good luck with your investigations and if you have to stay another night, I suggest you ask Helen if you can have her room and she can bunk in with her mom." She dabbed her lips with her serviette and rushed off in search of her pupil.

Gordon had not brought a spare uniform with him, and although he had a change of underwear and socks, he felt in desperate need of a good shower or bath. Going home for fresh clothes was not an option, the city of Pietermaritzburg where he lived was at least three hour's drive away.

The dust of the long drive was still caked in places he did not want to think about and the disturbed night had shaken him up quite badly and he was sure he could smell the sweat of fear on his body, so he went in search of the bathroom.

He collected a towel and some soap from Pamela at reception and in no time at all was lying soaking in a bath filled to the brim with hot water in the bathroom upstairs.

He had looked at the supply of bath salts on display and treated himself to a blend of sandalwood and lavender. The stress of the previous day melted away as he thought through his observations.

Steve, the lover was a non-starter. As were his cohorts. Who would have a motive? The van Rooyen family seemed genuinely distressed at Charlotte's death.

Motives came in the form of love, money or passion. Who benefitted from her dying? The aunt in Tongaat might have left an estate. But was it a large amount of money or property? A few phone calls were in order.

Getting out of the now cold water, Gordon planned out his day. An image of Helen came into his mind and he found himself smiling in anticipation of seeing her again.

CHAPTER SEVENTEEN

His ablutions were disturbed by a blood curdling scream. Throwing a towel around his waist he dashed out of the bathroom towards the noise.

He found Ruth looking with horror at her bed where a nasty looking knobkerrie lay amongst the covers. Bits of hair could be seen stuck to the vicious head of the fighting-stick. Congealed blood acted as a magnet for a series of blow flies buzzing around.

Ruth threw her arms around Gordon and buried her face in his bare shoulder clutching him tightly with her quivering arms as close as was humanly possible.

"I came in to get a book to read. Who would have done this? It's awful." Gordon could feel her tears wetting his chest as she sobbed for a moment. And then she suddenly went limp in his arms and fainted onto the floor.

She collapsed in an elegant heap in the most ladylike manner he had ever seen. Ruth had fallen softly sideways onto the thick carpet and as far as Gordon could see, she was uninjured. He quickly grabbed a cushion off a handy chair and elevated her legs slightly while he straightened her out making sure her airways were not obstructed and she was comfortable.

Fainting women seemed to abound in this hotel he thought. What he needed was a sensible head on intelligent shoulders to deal with this. Looking up he saw just the person he needed. Helen said, "Good morning Gordon. What have we here? A lady swooning at your manly breast?"

He looked down at his bare chest and the skimpy towel showing much too much flesh for a policeman on duty. "Just a sec Helen, I had better get dressed. Can you look after Ruth for me? She had a nasty shock."

Gordon quickly ran back to the bathroom and retrieved his shirt and pants before returning to find Ruth sitting up and looking a little bit more normal. He perched himself on the chair and proceeded to put on his shoes and socks.

Chapter Eighteen

Helen thought he looked very young with his hair sticking up all over the place from his hurried dressing. What on earth was he doing in Ruth's room in such a state of undress?

Gordon looked up at Helen and blushed. She wondered if he knew her thoughts and the assumptions about what she had witnessed. Ruth and Gordon had been seen whispering together at breakfast, maybe they had been making an assignation and things had gone bad.

But as Helen thought this she knew Gordon was not capable of anything bad. She felt a strange jealous tingle she had not felt for a while but she had to shrug it off as she turned to Ruth.

Gordon finished tying his shoelaces and said, "It's a good thing I was finished with my bath when you screamed Ruth." He grinned sheepishly at Helen as he offered this explanation of his state of undress.

Helen grinned back, oddly relieved to hear his simple excuse and then she turned to Ruth once more and said, "What happened Ruth? An intruder? What sent you into a faint?"

With eyes as wide as saucers and a shaking hand she pointed towards her bed. It was immediately apparent what had set Ruth off was no intruder, but rather the nasty looking fighting stick used by Zulu men called a knobkerrie.

The pristine white bedspread around the head of the knobkerrie was stained with a red mark looking a bit like strawberry jam but was not. The buzzing of the flies seemed to grow with each moment. A cursory glance was enough for Helen to add two and two together and know this was probably the murder weapon.

The nasty carved head was vicious enough to inflict a fatal head wound. Helen looked up to see Gordon calmly leaning against the door frame.

"Now where did the fighting stick come from Gordon? And why is it in Ruth's bedroom? Is someone trying to tell us something important or was it an act of impulse? And why did the murderer use a knobkerrie? I know there was a night watchman during the night, but what time did he go off duty?"

Helen listed the observations on her fingers. She looked at Gordon with his still wet hair and felt a small stirring of something warm inside her. She tucked his wayward collar under and allowed herself a moment to run her hands over his uniform in a possessive manner. He raised his eyebrows in query, but did not stop Helen as she straightened his shirt.

Ruth had risen and leaned against the passageway wall. "How dare some miscreant put a weapon on my bed? When I find out who the culprit is, I will give them an earful. Nasty people with nothing better to do than scare a poor girl half out of her wits. What sort of person would do such a thing?" She muttered to no one in particular. Her face transformed from white as a sheet to red as a beetroot as her blood pressure rose with her memory of what she had seen.

Helen put her arm around Ruth's shoulders and said, "Let's go and find a cup of coffee to warm you up and ease the shock. You are shaking all over, poor girl. Come along. Lean on me if you need to."

Gordon looked at the new evidence on Ruth's bed and called after Helen to send up the manager.

Delphinia arrived from a room further down the passage. "Miss Helen, Miss Ruth are you okay? I heard screaming but had to first finish cleaning the rooms before I could come."

She got to Ruth's bedroom door and let out a screech of her own. "Hau hau, who messed up such a nice bedspread? I just cleaned this room not an hour ago. The stick is Mr. van Rooyen's knobkerrie. I polished it just a few days ago. But it was hanging on his office wall last time I saw it. Oh, this is not good. First Miss Charlotte and now this mess," Delphinia lamented.

Gordon said, "This is getting a bit out of hand ladies. Helen if you could escort both Ruth and Delphinia downstairs I will be able to start my scene examination. And Helen, I will be down soon to take their statements." He smiled at her over his shoulder. Though she wanted to stay she left Gordon to his work.

CHAPTER NINETEEN

Helen sat in the lounge with a freshly brewed tea while the others talked over the morning's excitement. Ruth still looked a little pale as she said, "I taught Matilda for an hour, but she gets tired really easily and needed to have a lie down. I thought I might as well collect a book to read from my bedroom, only to find this abomination in the middle of my bed." Ruth looked at Delphinia. "Did you see anyone who might have put it there?"

Delphinia shook her head as she replenished the tray of pastries. "No one, Miss Ruth. I was in the rooms cleaning. But no one came down the passage. I'm sure I would have heard something."

Helen said, "Ada and I heard nothing either. We were getting ready to go for a walk to town. Mom wanted to buy some sweets to add to our hiking supplies. I was getting a hat out of the cupboard when I heard you screaming, Ruth. I certainly didn't see a soul on my way up the stairs or when we came out. What a mystery." Looking at the other two women she asked, "Who else has rooms on our floor?"

Ruth answered, "The Major and Mrs. Swindells-Smyth, myself, Fiona and yourselves. Pamela Meaker is staying in the room closest to the stairs." Looking up at the ceiling, she continued. "On the top floor are the four construction men from the jail, Charlotte and the van Rooyen family who have a small suite. Quite a houseful."

Delphinia took up the list of inhabitants adding, "On the ground floor near the pub are another three rooms but they are for the snooker table and gym. Constable Brown is in a room out the back and four other construction workers in the other two rooms built on to the back near the kitchen."

She looked at Helen as she said there was also a set of cabins further out the back housing other workers from the jail. "They look after themselves Miss Helen and only come into the hotel to drink and eat. Well we know the construction men and Sue the nurse, are out working, so it leaves ourselves, the van Rooyen family and the major and Maisie and Fiona who could have put the knobkerrie on the bed. It's just a matter of finding out where everyone was between breakfast the finding the weapon."

Ruth helpfully added, "I know Fiona was going to town after breakfast. She said she was going to visit Mary Markus for a coffee and a chat. Mary lives on the other side of the highway, in the nurses' home. Well, it used to be a nurses' home a few years back but is now a glorified boarding house. Mary is the landlady and Fiona and she often get together for a natter."

She suddenly stood up and said, "I will get Pamela to phone and find out if she is still there and if she has been there all morning."

Delphinia said, "I had better get back to work if I want to keep my job."

Helen sat for a while thinking things through when Pamela Meaker came into the lounge obviously surprised at the day's developments. "I overheard Ruth speaking to her sister. How awful to have her bedroom and privacy invaded. Poor girl must feel all shook up. I know I would. When we were bombed during the Blitz it was such attack on one's personal space, but this is much more intimate? Is there any tea going begging? I could do with a nice cup to sooth my nerves. I must say my nerves are shot since the war. Every little thing sets me off. I decided to get as far away from all the violence as I could. But it seems to have followed me regardless."

Pamela nervously played with her watch strap until Helen obligingly poured her a cup of tea. Her hands shook noticeably as she took a sip. Ada came to join them and sat quietly in the seat as Pamela lamented the war and how it had changed so much in her life. Her home in ruins, her only brother dead over the battlefields of France. Friends and family fragmented and some so badly affected they would never be the same again.

"Craig, my brother, was such a sweetheart. Always gentle and caring. Then he was in some awful air battle and from then on, he would shiver at the least little noise. Hated being in crowds. The last time I saw him lose his temper when some child popped a balloon near him. Not like Craig to be so nervy. He was usually the one to spend time with children. He was sent back to the front a week later. It was soon after the telegram came."

She got a faraway look in her eyes as she continued. "They brought the telegram to the office because there was no home address left to deliver it to. We watched the messenger come across the office floor and dreaded the thought it might be for one of us. And this time it was for me." She took another sip of her tea and then without another word, went back to her nice safe desk far away from devastating telegrams or destructive bombs and heart-breaking memories of a brother who would never grow old.

Ruth came back to report her sister had been at Mary's kitchen table for the past hour and a half and could not possibly have placed the knobkerrie on her bed. None of them had thought Fiona would have been the culprit. This didn't leave them many people to place in their suspect pool. Apart from the Major and Maisie, and it only left the staff to suspect. But what would be their motive? Surely none of them would want to kill Charlotte?

Ruth needed to return to her student and reluctantly climbed back up the stairs to report to Mrs. van Rooyen. Helen hated the dead ends in the investigation. Would they ever get closure for Charlotte? That had her following Pamela out to the reception area to ask some more questions.

"Pamela, what do you do at night? Do you lock up the hotel? And who has a set of keys." Helen leaned against the reception desk and grilled Pamela.

"Oh dear. I am sure there must be a reason why I shouldn't divulge this information, and I have been taught to keep my mouth zipped. But, if this will help you find the offender, then I am happy to help. It's not like in the war when loose lips sunk ships. Those days are behind us, so tell me again what you need to know? I know Simeon was on guard duty most of the night, but he knocked off just after dawn," She continued mumbling to herself as she opened drawers in search of what she wanted.

She found the register of keys. The system was not exactly robust and a determined killer would have had no problem coming and going. There was a spare set of front door keys inside the cupboard under the stairs. Kept there in the event of a fire and a need for people to escape.

Pamela tutted and drew up a new key register to reflect the modern-day custodians. None of this helped Helen with the investigations.

Ada came in from her trip to the shops and joined Helen in the lounge. "Mom, while you were out someone dropped the murder weapon in the middle of Ruth's bed. No one saw a thing of course. I'm beginning to think it is ghosts playing tricks."

She laughed at this absurd idea. "No, of course not. But it's a little bit confusing to say the least. Let's see if the ladies lounge is open. We'll think better with a cold drink in hand." They wandered off to find a cool drink while they discussed their next step.

Mr. van Rooyen and Gordon could be heard in the office discussing how someone could have removed his knobkerrie from the wall. Gordon stuck his head around the doorjamb and called Helen over to get her camera and join them. Helen didn't need to be invited twice. Ada happily waved her off and retreated to a corner to read her book.

A bell rang somewhere in the hotel and Mr. van Rooyen went off to supervise his guests leaving the two alone in the office.

Helen removed the cap of the camera once she had retrieved it from her room. "Now Gordon, what have you found out since we met this morning? Who has a motive and who has an alibi, because for the life of me, I am flummoxed." Helen smiled sheepishly at her admission. He pointed to the wall where he wanted her to take a photo. There were hooks on the wall to hold the knobkerrie.

"Helen flummoxed? We must do all we can to solve this murder so dear Helen need not be confused any more. But sorry, my dear girl, I don't have a clue.

No motive I can discern. No suspect has appeared from the woodwork. I am surprised. You always seem to know everything, so how is it you are as befuzzled as I am?"

She put down the camera once she had the shot of the space where the knobkerrie came from. Glancing at Gordon she could see the mirth dancing in his eyes.

"Don't tease Gordon. There are times when I don't know everything. Let's make a few lists, shall we? After we have a clear picture of all the people in the hotel it might help you solve the murder and me to be less befuzzled." Helen teased Gordon right back.

"And then we can go to lunch and afterwards I'm going to have a nap, and we can see if my subconscious mind comes up with the answer after forty winks. You are no help at all Gordon. How is it you, a trained policeman, are less informed than I am. It makes no sense at all."

Chapter Twenty

Helen pored over a list of guests and staff for the remainder of the morning, crossing names out and making copious notes with Gordon. At the end of the hour no conclusion was reached. Everyone had an alibi and no one seemed to have a motive.

"Gordon, I don't envy you at all. This puzzle seems to have no solution at all. Not a single person seems to have wanted Charlotte dead. Good luck with finding your murderer," Helen said as she rose up and readied herself for her lunch. She put her hand on Gordon's arm and they walked out together and collected Ada from the lounge as they wandered towards the dining room.

As they sat down to a lunch of cold meats and salads, Ada commented. "This holiday is perfect, Helen. The food is fantastic, the scenery spectacular and the accommodation comfortable. Just a pity Charlotte is not here to enjoy it with us."

"Yes Mom, I agree. Delicious food, I am going to have to let my dresses out somewhat once I get home," Helen said as she dipped her spoon into her dessert.

Helen licked her lips after enjoying the lemon meringue pie and thought she would have no trouble falling asleep, her brain needed a rest and her full stomach would no doubt facilitate this desire. Gordon was looking through their notes and Ada had risen and wandered away to talk to Maisie. Helen wandered up to her room for a nap and Helen hoped Charlotte would visit and enlighten her a bit more in her dreams. She didn't want to mention her special gift to Gordon, but Ada was fully aware of the family inheritance of what was called, second sight amongst those in the know. The journey from dining room to bedroom was slow as Helen pondered all the things that they day had brought.

Wisp was at the door of the room when Helen entered and complained bitterly at not having another stroll through the gardens. Helen sighed and picked up her pet and its harness before going downstairs. The pub and dining room were empty and only Pamela could be seen filing papers in Mr. van Rooyen's office. The sun was shining and it was a perfect day to spend outside.

Helen walked down the stairs towards the little stream. She glimpsed an orchard across a rickety bridge past some spreading chestnut trees. The rose garden was much too exposed and sunny for a snooze and she went on a wander of discovery through the grounds.

A grove of trees along the boundary fence looked promising. Branches hung low over sun dappled glades. She found a shady bench under the trees and tying Wisp's harness to her arm, she leaned back and closed her eyes.

A gentle breeze lifted the hair off her forehead and soothed her as it tickled her softly with its warm fingers. The bench was a rustic construction of time worn timbers and was perfectly shaped for relaxing.

She felt the air move as someone sat on the bench next to her and Helen opened her eyes to see who it could be, but there was no one there at all. This had never happened before, a ghost manifesting themselves to her while she was still awake.

Wisp wound herself around her legs and then sat down on Helen's other side, not in the least disturbed by the spirit's presence. Wisp turned around a few times and then purred loudly as she settled down.

Helen leaned back in the cool of the shady trees and closed her eyes once more and allowed the peace of the garden to lull her into a doze. Even the birds and the cicadas stilled their noise.

Sleep descended as it always did with its velvet touch on her conscious mind. The sounds of the breeze were almost hypnotic as waves and Helen slipped into her doze. Darkness surrounded her and she realised she was not alone. She felt herself being led by the hand through a mist and into a light and spacious glade.

The crying man in his burning building was still there, as were the Zulu warriors, but they were not coming forward or demanding attention. The ghost dog sat quietly and Helen leaned down to pat its head as she was walking and its tail thumped on the ground in joy. Its sad eyes lit up and it followed her into the field of flowers.

Helen turned to Charlotte next to her and looked past her and to her surprise, saw many more apparitions filling the space. As far as she could see there were people ancient and modern, observing them.

She saw a family of ancient Africans whose hands were stained with pigments and she wondered if they were the creators of the rock paintings in the area. A family of Boers stood with their oxen alongside their covered wagons.

Helen could feel each of their spirits filled with love and concern for Charlotte. None of the apparitions moved towards them and Helen was able to ignore them all and focus on her friend.

Charlotte twirled around in a gossamer dress and sparkly shoes, dancing gaily through the flowers. "Charlotte, I need to talk to you. Who killed you? We can't find any clues to who it was," Helen asked as she grasped at Charlotte's arm.

Charlotte stopped twirling and whispered, "My Mother. Find my Mother, and you will find the culprit."

"Charlotte, who is your Mother? Where do I find her?" Helen begged as Charlotte started to fade.

But she was fading fast. Dancing amongst the other ghosts. Charlotte turned around for a moment and blew Helen a kiss. "Mama, why didn't you love me, Mama?"

The crying man grasped at Helen's hand as she stood looking after the murdered girl. The Zulu warriors came closer and she was not in the least scared as they too touched her hands and arm. Soft as a feather they surrounded her and drew her closer and closer. She could feel their sadness and their angst.

The crying man had a puddle of tears at his feet and said, "All the tears in the world and nothing will stop the flames. I lost it all. My dream, my life, my future. Now I sit here gnashing my teeth at my choices. You have a great life ahead of you. Don't let it pass you by."

A Zulu warrior started licking her wrist and she didn't think it strange at all in her dreamlike state. She smiled at the crying man and hugged each warrior in turn until it was just the arm licking warrior left. She turned to him and took him in her arms and hugged him as he too started to weep.

The glade around her shimmered and the ghosts stepped back into the time between their world and the one inhabited by Helen.

Chapter Twenty-One

Helen woke up with Wisp licking her arm. Wisp immediately jumped off the bench as soon as Helen opened her eyes and pulled on the harness until her mistress got the hint and stood up.

"What was that all about?" She mumbled to herself as she stood looking around her at the trees, the burbling brook and the innocuous insects going about their business.

Gordon smiled as he strode across the lawn.

"Helen, I have been looking all over for you. I thought you were in your bedroom and here I find you swanning around in the wilderness." He leaned down to scratch Wisp under the chin. "Aaah, I see. Young mistress Wisp needed an ablution walkie."

"Gordon, was there anything you needed to tell me? Why were you looking for me? A new clue? Someone confess? Or even better you have figured it all out and wanted to share your discovery with me?" She went down on her haunches to be eye to eye with him and she too scratched the cat's fur.

"Oh, yes. No, I haven't found anything new to tell you. But the boss in Pietermaritzburg has suggested I return to the office and work from there for a while as I'm making very little progress here in Bulwer. I have come to say goodbye," Gordon said as he rose to his feet.

She too straightened. Bringing Wisp up as well in her arms. "Okay, but my sub-conscious has said to look at her family. We know she was adopted by her aunt, but I think it's worth pursuing her parentage.

No one here seems to have any motive for killing her off, so the next stop is relatives." She placed Wisp on the bench she had recently vacated. Gordon placed a warm hand on her arm.

"Really Helen, where do you get these ideas from? We would have known if a relative was responsible. But, okay, okay, I will see what I can find. The archives in the city will have her birth certificate with her real mother on it. I can sneak over there in my lunch break and see what I can find. But now, I must dash. Long drive and all it entails. Be a sweetheart and don't go poking where you are not wanted. Leave it to us professionals."

He leaned over and gave her a peck on the cheek. A fleeting wish wanted him to move the kiss to her lips but she pushed it away as he drew her into a brief hug. She felt his strong arms ready to release her and decided she didn't want him to go.

Grasping his lapels, she pulled him back and gave him a light kiss on his lips.

"Drive carefully. Your motor bike looks dangerous and I do worry about you." Helen kissed him lightly again.

Gordon gathered her to his chest and kissed the top of her head as he whispered, "And I worry about you too, Sweetheart. Don't go asking people questions. It is my job. Just enjoy your holiday. I will keep in touch. Bye."

He smoothed a hand over Wisp's head before he wandered off over the lawn to where his bike was waiting on the road.

"Mmm, Wisp. What do you make of Gordon thinking we need to be kept safe? As if I would poke my nose anywhere it was not appreciated." Helen winked at her cat and the two of them walked back to the hotel.

At reception she found her mother talking to Pamela. "Helen look at this. A famous artist is giving art workshops at the old mission home down the road. Maybe we should take the day off tomorrow and do something productive? It starts at nine in the morning, so we still have the afternoon to do a bit of a walk today if we want to. Across the highway to the new jail and then to visit Mary at her boarding house. We should be back before it gets dark and will help to clear our minds of all this drama."

"Sure Mom, I will take Wisp upstairs and find a nice pair of walking shoes and a sensible hat to cover my head. No good me getting more freckles to add to the multitude already covering my face. Won't be a minute," Helen said.

Chapter Twenty-Two

Picking Wisp up under her arm, Helen took off up the stairs in search of sensible attire. When she returned her Mother and Pamela were still chatting about the painting session the next day.

Perla Gibson was an opera singer who also dabbled in painting. "So sad to hear her son died in the war. And she still went and sang to the departing and returning troops in Durban harbour on the very day she received the news. Such a brave woman. Many a young man was affected by her dedication. I know my nephew said he had been uplifted by her singing. She stood in the middle of Durban harbour and sang through a loud hailer. Amazing."

Seeing Helen descending the staircase, Ada stopped speaking and turned to smile at her daughter. "All ready? Good. I have a backpack filled with eats and drinks to tide us over. Young Musa was very helpful. Bye Pamela." She said as they waved goodbye and stepped out into the afternoon sunshine.

Nothing was said until they had forded the stream and were on the slight uphill towards town. "Did your snooze give you any answers?" Ada asked Helen.

Helen proceeded to tell her Mother about her strange encounter with the different ghosts. They both agreed the licking of the arm was perhaps a response to Wisp's administrations in the real world and not likely to be of any consequence.

The burning man was also not very helpful towards discovering the murderer. His story was the one Mrs. Van Rooyen had spoken of with the death of the first owner of the hotel. This left Charlotte and her declaration of parental involvement. Helen told Ada about Gordon's promise to look into the birth certificate.

"Okay my dear child, nothing much more we can do at the moment, let us get those legs of yours working. Come on let's go a bit faster along this bit." Ada urged Helen as they crossed the small stream.

They crossed the highway and up a dusty track towards the construction site on the rise. The men were downing tools for afternoon tea as they arrived and they were able to sit down and join them all.

Steve made a point of not sitting with them, but Sam and Johan were happy to sit and chat and sneak a bite or two of the delicious cheese scones Musa had packed.

They joked and laughed and spoke about a dance they were going to in Underberg on Friday. They spoke about girls they had met and teased each other about the possibility of being kissed under the moonlight.

"Who would want to kiss an ugly guy like you Johan? Maybe someone with glasses as thick as milk bottles?" Sam dodged a punch from his friend as they laughed uproariously. Realistically the number of girls far outnumbered the men available and both Johan and Sam could have the pick of the bunch if they so wanted.

Johan had developed a taste for foreign travel during the war and said, "I saw Egypt and the pyramids. Do you know, I loved all the foreign food and the different languages? Like something out of a storybook. When I marry, it will be to a girl who will not want children right away but be happy to see the world first. Egypt, with a boat ride up the Nile. Then across to Italy with all its beautiful statues. I went swimming off the coast while we were there. There were even marble statues under the ocean. I don't know if I want to go to England. Too cold for my taste, but certainly, France would be fun. I have no interest in Germany. Those Nazis put me off going there. I might even go to Australia and meet up with those mates I met in the war. Kangaroos will make a nice change from our African animals. Yup, can't wait to travel. I am working to earn enough for a ticket and then I am off to discover the world."

"Nah, no travel for me. I want a pretty little blonde who can please me in b…" Sam stopped speaking and looked sheepishly at Ada and Helen. "Oops, sorry ladies. It just kind of slipped out."

The conversation soon turned to the murder and both men had plenty to say about it. They thought it might be an intruder of some sort and neither of the women corrected them in their assumptions. Gert came over and sat with them but didn't say a word apart from a short greeting for the women.

Johan asked, "Gert, are you coming to the dance with us this weekend? A little bit of window shopping for a fine lady friend? I know you enjoy dancing. I've seen you do a little twirl when you are getting ready for bed at night."

"Nee. I am not in the mood for a party, Johan. I'll leave all the pretty girls to you two and I might go and visit my brother and see how he is doing. Thanks for asking me but not this time," Gert replied.

CHAPTER TWENTY-THREE

Tea break was soon over and Steve called the men back to work. Helen reluctantly went on her way, armed with a map of the town. They found their way to the boarding house, which turned out to be an old house with an outside bathroom and kitchen tacked onto the back of the home.

They had never met Mary before, but she happily invited them inside. Fiona was already sitting at the kitchen table and sipping a cup of coffee as they walked in.

"Well fancy meeting you here?" She quipped. "What have you been up to? Flirting with the quite delectable looking constable? Or just relaxing?"

Helen had never considered Gordon as being delectable, but she could see how Fiona had come to the conclusion. He did have the most amazing grey eyes that pierced your deepest thoughts.

"Actually, the constable has returned to his office in Pietermaritzburg and Mom and I have been for a walk to the new jail. Tomorrow we are going to the Mill for a lesson in art by Perla Gibson. We are both enjoying our holiday no end," Helen added.

Mary leaned in closer. "Perla Gibson? I thought she was an opera singer? My brother and fiancé wrote letters to me saying how marvellous she was. You are so fortunate to be able to spend some time learning from her. I do hope the weather stays fine for you. Now, how about a nice cup of tea or coffee before you have to trudge over the road and up the hill?"

They sat out on the veranda and marvelled at the lovely view they had of the mountains and even the odd cart or car trundling down the highway.

Helen had no need to try and get information out of Mary, she spoke non-stop about everything under the sun. Strange guests, speeding vehicles and bumps in the night, followed by an insight into who was sleeping with whom in the district.

Old Mrs. Parsons who looked like she was harmless, was a cougar on the prowl and the bane of every serviceman in the area. No electrician or plumber would venture anywhere near her. They had devised a system of taking along an apprentice if they were forced to visit her.

Mary laughed as she said, "There was a new electrician who didn't know of Mrs. Parson's proclivity for fresh men to hunt. The boss thought the kid would be safe because Mr. Parsons was home and yet the old dear still managed to have a good feel before the youngster took off running down the driveway, never to be seen again. The boss heard from him two days later when he reached Howick. The kid said if this was what he would have to put up with then he might as well get a job selling clothes in a men's outfitters. Poor kid got a lesson in old ladies and their sex drives."

Helen laughed until her sides hurt imagining the event. As the sun started dipping down, Mary said, "I need to start cooking the evening meal before my guests arrive. Sorry ladies, I'll have to throw you out unless you would prefer to do the cooking for me. It's tripe and onions for dinner tonight."

The three women declined the invite to do the cooking and left her to stroll back to the hotel, laughing at their shared afternoon of entertainment.

But Helen couldn't get her encounter with the ghosts from her mind so turned the conversation to a more serious note.

"Fiona do you know who Charlotte's parents were? I know you and your sister said she was brought up in Tongaat, but did she ever say anything about her birth parents?"

Fiona was thoughtful before she answered. "Yes, she said something one day surprising me a bit. She said her mother had been married and while her husband was away overseas, the mother had an affair with the local butcher. Before the husband returned, Charlotte was born and shipped off to the maiden aunt. She said she never met her mother except once when she was about ten. Her mother came to visit her aunt with her two sons. The boys were both teenagers and the whole time they were there, no one mentioned the fact they were actually, half siblings. It was only when they left the aunt let slip the boys were in fact her brothers. Strange. Not knowing your mother." Fiona shrugged her shoulders as she divulged this piece of gossip to Helen.

Ada brought the conversation to something light and asked Fiona a question. Fiona jumped on the opportunity to speak about herself. This allowed Helen to mull over the sad tale of Charlotte and her mother.

Much as Helen loved her brothers, they did tease her and at times she wished she might have a holiday from them, but not to have a family would be even worse.

They arrived at the hotel to find Maisie leaning over the reception counter talking to Pamela. "I have wanted to visit the Reichenau Mission, do you think I could register for this painting group tomorrow?"

"Of course, Mrs. Swindells-Smythe there are plenty of spaces left in the group. Aah, here are the Bell ladies. Maybe they would be able to oblige with a ride in their car to the venue?" Pamela turned to Helen and waited for her acceptance.

Ada answered for Helen even though she would be the driver. "Maisie, how perfect. We can sit side by side and paint to our heart's content. I am not any good at painting, but a day out surrounded by lovely old buildings and pretty scenery will be fantastic. We can leave the serious art stuff to Helen and the tutor, Perla."

Helen went off to wash her hands before dinner as Maisie filled her name on the sign-up sheet.

CHAPTER TWENTY-FOUR

Dinner was a quiet affair without Gordon to talk to. Ruth and Fiona sat at a double table and the rest of the company seemed preoccupied with their own thoughts. Maisie and the major sat at the table adjacent to the Bells and Maisie kept on leaning over to say an odd word or two all evening.

Helen decided not to go to the ladies lounge after dinner, but rather took Wisp for a walk around the gardens in the twilight while Ada sat on a bench and read her book.

As the sun set the hotel took on a particular beauty. Windows gleaming with light and lamps along the paths created a magical feeling. For the first time since they had arrived, Helen felt the peace seep into her soul.

She thought of David and how much he would have enjoyed the walk. Not for the first time, Helen wondered why her fiancé had never visited her in her dreams. The night after he was killed and long before she was notified of his death, she had felt someone sit on the edge of her bed and touch her forehead in a gentle kiss. Nothing more and nothing since then.

What was the use of having a gift of seeing dead if she couldn't see the one she most wanted to be with?

Even the memory of David's face was fading and she had to think hard to remember what he had been like.

She collected a book from the hotel bookcase and went upstairs to spend a quiet night in their rooms.

As soon as her mother had retired, Helen dressed in a pair of dark pants and a black shirt. She hoped her clothing would make her invisible as she went in pursuit of more information.

With a torch hidden in her hand she crept up to Charlotte's room and gently tried the handle. It would not budge and then Helen remembered Gordon had the key and had locked the room behind him once the body had been removed.

Pulling a hair clip from her hair, she twisted it into the lock. It had been a while since she had done this. The last time had been at St Cuthbert's school for girls when matron had refused to give her the food parcel her parents had sent to her. That time she had been caught red handed and punished severely for her flaunting of the rules of the hostel.

Helen hoped this night would not be a repeat of the time in the matron's office. She had no wish to be discovered scratching through Charlotte's papers.

The lock clicked open and Helen slipped inside and pulled the door closed behind her. Not wanting to alert anyone to her presence, she did not switch on the light. She knew the door did not reach right to the floor and had no wish for someone to see the sliver of light and come to investigate.

Taking her torch in hand she started her search. First under the bed. A box filled with photographs was a good start and Helen sat on the bed as she quickly rummaged through them.

Photos of Charlotte with an older lady on the beach. A studio portrait of Charlotte all dressed up in a ball-gown. A few photos of Charlotte as a young girl on a horse, more with her and boys of all ages. None of the boys looked familiar and there were none showing her with her mother. But still Helen thought they might be worth a closer look.

She tipped the contents of the box into her backpack.

A noise outside the room had Helen looking for a hiding place. A shuffle of feet on the landing and a furtive twist of the door handle had the blood pounding in her head.

She switched off the torch and held her breath in anticipation of discovery. She could not see anywhere suitable to hide and had to hope if the person entered they might not switch on the light. She stood against the wall behind the door and waited.

Helen felt a drip of sweat slide down her backbone and she breathed slowly in and out in an attempt to control her breath. The door handle was twisted and the door opened just enough to allow a shadowy person to enter.

The box holding the photographs was still lying on the bed, empty, and the intruder looked at it for a moment before opening the drawers next to the bed and tipping their contents out.

Helen could not see the features of the person, but the shape seemed very masculine. Tall and slim with wide shoulders he was carefully sorting through the things on the bed and Helen took the opportunity to slip quietly out the door while he was distracted.

Careful not to make any noise, she hoped none of the floor boards would creak as she made her escape.

Helen waited in the shadows of the passage to see if she could recognise the intruder when he came out of the room. He exited a few minutes later and walked down the passage away from Helen not even looking over his shoulder.

The shadowy man descended the stairs and she waited a while longer to be sure he was gone before Helen re-entered Charlotte's bedroom.

The bed was strewn with an assortment of costume jewellery and knick knacks had been ripped from the cupboards. Taking her time to sort them carefully, Helen replaced what she could into the drawers. It didn't seem right not to show respect for Charlotte's possessions and make sure they were as she would have wanted them.

Helen didn't find any letters or paperwork to help her in her quest and an hour later she was back in her room. The photos yielded little of interest and Helen promised herself she would return them to Charlotte's room as soon as she could safely do it. She felt quite disappointed at the lack of information amongst Charlotte's things.

Chapter Twenty-Five

Finally settled in bed Helen's dreams were undisturbed and she arose feeling refreshed, but surprised. Charlotte had not pestered her to find her killer.

In the early morning, she took Wisp for a quick walk while she thought of the intruder who had broken into Charlotte's room the night before. What had they been looking for? If it was the killer had he left something behind that could incriminate him? She hadn't seen anything in his hands but the shadows had hidden everything but his presence.

She had to put it out of her mind as she met her mother and the others in the reception area. Ready for their drive and art class.

The drive to Reichenau was pleasant as the two older ladies commented on the children walking to school alongside the highway. "Look at them Ada. Cute as buttons and off to school walking for miles to get an education. We need to give them some sort of reward," Maisie declared.

Helen was asked to stop so the ladies could throw out a handful of pennies and sweeties. Feeling generous because of their largesse, the car carried on, smothered in clouds of dust as the children strolled along to their rural schools happily chewing at the unexpected sugary treats and counting out their pennies in anticipation of even more treats.

Reichenau looked spectacular in the early morning light. Old stone buildings alongside a picturesque stream and backed by impressive hills and distant mountains had the ladies oohing and aahing.

"Oh goodness me Maisie, I might even be inspired to paint something with this scenery as inspiration," Ada announced. Mist still lay in the wisps along the riverbed and clung to some of the trees as the sun did its best to disperse it.

Perla was ready to welcome the artists. Dressed in a flowing white dress and topped off with a large brimmed hat trimmed with fresh flowers and looking exotic, she smiled at each newcomer as they arrived. "Welcome fellow artists. Welcome to my humble class." Perla waved her red tipped fingers at each and every artist. She blew kisses at the monks on their way to their daily labours. They shuffled shyly away from the effusive woman who had invaded their domain.

There were others from the district who had already arrived. Sturdy farmer's wives, the wife of a retired solicitor, and even a couple of French tourists travelling through the district had joined the group.

Perla was very efficient in her instructions of where to sit and what to do. Within a few minutes the artists were told to stand and introduce themselves to the others.

"Hi, my name is Perla and I am not only an artist, but an opera singer too. I live in Durban and I'm a very happy person, usually. Now it is your turn to introduce yourself. We will start in the corner over there," Perla said as she pointed to a slim woman dressed in a twin set wool outfit with a gold chain around her neck and flashy diamond rings on all her fingers.

"Hi, my name is Marsha and I live in Ixopo with my husband and three teenage children."

And so, it continued. Sara a farmer's wife, Francois, a French soldier and Melanie, the French soldier's wife. Petra, the wife of a solicitor and Katharina, a sheep farmer. Maria, a catholic nun And Jacoba, a rather shy woman who introduced herself as, "Jacoba, but my life is not as interesting as any of you people. I just like to paint."

Perla glided through the room. Her hands pressed together. "Good. Good. Now look at the paints and brushes in front of you, those are for you to use. We will start with a simple painting of an old door at the end of the building. I have supplied you with a board prepared with Gesso. Use the pencil supplied to draw the door on the board. It doesn't matter where you place it."

She then walked around behind each student and suggested minor adjustments. A little to the left, a bit bigger, or smaller. Composition and lighting. By ten o'clock the artists had all drawn a basic outline and simple details.

A tray of tea, coffee and lemonade was brought around by a Trappist monk. Another monk carried a tray of sandwiches and small cakes. The monks kept their heads well down as they delivered their offering to the guests.

The artists took the break time to observe the other drawings as they wandered round with drink in one hand and snack in the other.

Perla joined in the observations. She stopped next to Maisie and said, "I know you. Didn't our sons go to the same school in Durban? On the Bluff? Yes, I remember you now. Your husband was in the army and during World War One both of our husbands were sent off to serve overseas. Terrible time for us young mothers. All alone with our children. Times were tough."

Maisie smiled at Perla. Maisie looked around to make sure everyone around them had heard the conversation. Happy to think she knew this famous lady and they had so much in common and some of the gloss of Perla was now hers to share. The two of them chatted for a moment.

"I remember you well Perla, you were always such a lovely lady. To think you have become so famous and I knew you when we were both just young women. I am thrilled to see you again. Just imagine how much our lives have changed," Maisie twittered.

The two women spoke about husbands at war and raising children on very little money. Having to stay stalwart and strong in the face of financial and personal challenges.

"Yes Maisie, we are the true heroes to have kept the home fires burning while never knowing if our men would ever return. Tough times, but we survived." Perla looked sad as she patted Maisie on the shoulder.

Perla looked at her watch and then started singing "When Irish eyes are smiling." In her beautiful clear voice. As everyone stopped talking to listen to her, she smiled and mid verse, she stopped and said, "Back to work my fellow artists. Come, come the day is passing too fast and life is short."

The day flew by and by the end of it they all had a passable painting in oil to take home and a better painting in water colours to cherish along with their memories of a day with the inimitable Perla.

Jacoba had surprised them all by producing an excellent set of art works. A really delicate touch had created a doorway into a magical kingdom for the first painting. An even more delicate watercolour of the mill stream was so beautiful Marsha pressed Jacoba to sell it to her for any price she wished to charge.

"Ag nee, you can just have it free. I can't ask for money for something I have enjoyed painting. It's a gift from me to you," She whispered humbly.

"What? No, this will not do," Interjected Perla. "An artist is worth their weight in gold, my dear girl. Do not sell yourself short. A painting like this, well, let me tell you in Durban you could get a nice sum of money. Don't give it away. Marsha name a price and I will tell you if I think it is a suitable amount."

With a bit of haggling the price was set and both Marsha and Jacoba went away happy with their sale and purchase.

The French soldier and his wife were to stay a few more days at Reichenau Mission camping in an old army surplus tent alongside the millstream. They hoped to work alongside the monks for their keep.

The rest of the people slowly dispersed into vehicles of different vintages. Maria the nun, was to catch a train from Underberg the following morning and was to sleep at the mission. The monks would be going to town by donkey cart in time for the train departure in the morning and would happily give Maria a lift to the station.

Helen, Ada and Maisie waved goodbye to their fellow artists and as the sun dropped in the sky, they drove to the hotel in time for dinner. No little school children on the road at the end of the day, but rather, there were people trudging home with large parcels strapped to their heads.

Zulu women with babies tied to their backs and often a toddler tagging along behind, were burdened with loads worthy of the strength of the strongest man. Young boys could be seen herding cows on distant hills as they found shelter for the night for themselves and their charges.

One old Zulu lady stopped her trudging and stood quietly observing the car disappear amongst the dust cloud. Her eyes holding a light to them that had Helen glancing at her again as they drove past.

CHAPTER TWENTY-SIX

On returning to the hotel at Bulwer, the three ladies unloaded their paintings and proudly showed them to Pamela at reception. Mr. van Rooyen insisted they display their art works along the side of the lounge area for everyone to admire.

The major diplomatically chose his wife's work as being the best, but the rest of the company were happy to buy free drinks to the hard-working ladies. Sam offered to pay for a bottle of the best champagne. Sadly, there was no champagne in the cellar and they had to settle for sparking grape juice.

Mr. van Rooyen suggested the pictures should be put in the ladies lounge overnight to dry. He offered the three ladies a gift of Swiss chocolates, and they all happily accepted the chocolates and the offer of displaying their work. They were pleased with what they had achieved.

Helen looked at her work and wondered if she might take this talent one step further and sell her paintings. She might not be as good as Perla, but she was pleased with her efforts. It certainly would solve her problem with finding work.

It was no surprise after eating chocolates late at night Helen's sleep should be filled with strange dreams. Charlotte came and sat on the edge of the bed and gently pulled at Helen's toe to get her attention.

"Hello, hello sleepy head. You spent the day with Mama Dearest. What did you find out?"

"Charlotte, I don't even know who your mother is, let alone find out anything of use. Leave me alone, I need to sleep."

But Charlotte insisted on sitting on the bed and talking about days in Tongaat with Auntie Margareta. Monkeys in trees, star fish in rock pools and a myriad of other childhood memories.

Till finally Helen said, "It looks like your childhood was a lovely time. Even without your mother around, you were well cared for and loved. I have seen your photos and you looked happy. What has this got to do with your murder? Auntie Margareta is dead because I can see her standing in the shadows behind you. Why were you killed? Money?"

Charlotte laughed and shook her head. "I have no money. But I wanted Mama to pay for all the years of neglect. The times Auntie Margareta begged her to write me a letter or send me a gift, no matter how small, and it was all too much trouble. I wanted her to pay for how she made me feel, unloved, thrown away and discarded."

Wisp hissed at the apparition and Helen sensed her cat as it insinuated itself into her dream. She saw an angry leopard poised and looking at Charlotte. Strangely enough Helen felt no fear at the menace of the predator, but rather a sense of protection and peace.

Charlotte backed away and her aunt stepped forward to offer support. "You have no idea what my sister is like. She looks gentle and sweet, but she has no compassion for flesh of her flesh. She is too concerned that the pencil of history will mark her as a scarlet woman. It's about pride and keeping her façade of respectability intact. She has no honour," Auntie Margareta declared.

The angry outburst surprised Helen and the leopard sprang forward towards the two women. In a wisp of smoke, they both disappeared and the leopard changed into a gentle kitten.

Helen felt the purring through her sleep and she relaxed back into a dreamless slumber for the remainder of the night.

Chapter Twenty-Seven

The following day was Sunday and many of the hotel guests walked across the highway to the little Yellowwood church for services. Helen and Ada strolled arm in arm along with the others dressed in their Sunday best. Their best being homemade dresses and sensible shoes.

They both sported hats designed and made by a real Russian duchess who had fallen on hard times and now had a business in the millinery trade. Each year the Bell women would buy a summer creation and a winter one to add to their growing collection.

Ada's hat was a vision of rose petals interspersed with butterflies and bees. While Helen's was more tailored and sensible. The austerity of the war years was behind them and they could happily wear their outfits with pride.

Ruth and Fiona both wore skirts slightly flared and puffed up with multiple petticoats and topped with blouses reminiscent of a man's shirt, but not like any male attire the Bell women had ever seen before. They too wore hats, but these resembled a French beret.

Sue and Pamela were in very austere tailored suits. The men were almost unrecognisable in button down shirts and dress trousers. Only the major wore a uniform while Maisie wore a dress with more frills than should ever be allowed on one outfit. She looked like a marshmallow puff and Helen felt quite sorry for her as Maisie looked so uncomfortable in her get up.

She pulled at the frills around her neck and kept tugging at her waist with its tiny belt.

The congregation entered the lynch gate and wove their way through the tomb stones of the grave-yard and down the path towards the little yellowwood church. Inside was simplicity itself with wooden pews and raw wood walls and roof.

Helen ran her hand appreciatively along the railing as she found her seat. The ceiling soared high above their heads shone with the glow of the yellowwood and the altar was covered with a hand-made lace cover showings signs of wear and had obviously seen better days. Light streamed through the arched windows and competed with the high chandelier casting its gentle light upon the people gathered below.

It might not look like some of the fine cathedrals of the world but a sweet spirit embellished the humble church with all the beauty any congregant could desire.

An organ played and an old man entered to the strains of the ancient tune, clothed in the robes of his ministerial office. The service was short and the hymns were sung with gusto by one and all. A few great baritone voices almost lifted the roof. Ruth had a surprisingly fine soprano and Fiona a decent alto.

Even the sermon had been interesting as the quivering voice of the minister had spoken of forty years in the wilderness. He compared the Israelite journey to World War Two and the need for faith in each person's life.

As far as Helen could see, no one had nodded off during the sermon and she had seen a few people nodding in agreement with the minister's sentiments.

Sacraments were served and collection taken. Prayers were said and hymns were sung.

Helen felt cleansed from the dramas of the week and ready for whatever life should throw at her.

The sunlight was brighter than expected as the congregation exited the church. The minister shook all their hands and thanked them for attending. Just outside the lynch gate Helen was surprised to see Gordon sitting on his motorbike.

"Care to come for a short ride with me fair maiden?"

"Oh Gordon, you are a sight for sore eyes. I would love to go for a short ride." Helen agreed as she rushed forward.

Throwing her mother a smile and a brief wave, Helen was careful to arrange her skirt as she swung her leg over the seat. She had to grab on to Gordon's waist as the bike roared off in a haze of dust.

The wind whipped her hair and she held onto her hat with one hand. They didn't travel far before Gordon pulled the bike off onto a grassy verge. A small stream chuckled its way over a rocky bottom and willow trees threw shadows over the bank.

Alongside the stream were soft sandy beaches and gentle banks offering tempting places to rest.

Pulling a blanket out of his saddle bags, Gordon laid it down on the still damp grass and helped Helen to dismount and settle on it.

"Well, I found Charlotte's birth certificate. Her mother is listed as Cornelia Catharina Magdalena Blignaut. Father is listed as Frank Fisher, butcher of Bluff in Durban. Written in pencil is the notation of bastard next to Charlotte's name. Her full name is Charlotte Margareta Cooper. No explanation of why she has a different name to her parents. We were lucky there were no official adoption papers. It looks like she was given to the aunt to bring up with no legal paperwork. If she was adopted we might never have been able to find the mother's name. Not much help in her murder I am afraid. The bosses are not pleased with me. It was supposed to be a simple investigation."

Gordon leaned over and removed a curl of hair from Helen's cheek and for a second, she lost her train of thought as she felt the world stop around them. He looked deep into her eyes and dropped his hand from her face to her arm and gently rubbed his thumb against the gooseflesh springing up on her body.

"Sorry Helen, are you cold?" Gordon pulled off his jacket and draped it around her shoulders. The warmth of his body still lingering in the folds. "Better? Sorry, where were we? Aah yes right, I have hit a brick wall in this investigation. I hope you have been enjoying your holiday and not looking into Charlotte's death. I know you Helen, you find it difficult to leave a good mystery alone. But trust me, this is no game. Leave it to us people who know what they are doing. I will unearth the culprit using tried and true methods of investigation. It might take a while, but I will get there eventually. Trust me."

Helen wasn't really cold but she pulled the jacket closer around her. Her fingers playing with the seam at the cuff. "Well Gordon, we did find out a few helpful things. Neither of us are trying to do investigating, but you might find them interesting. We went and spoke to Mary at the boarding house to find out if Fiona was really there when the knobkerrie was placed on Ruth's bed."

She let out a sigh. "She had been so it wasn't her. Not that I think she could have done such a thing. I'm not sure where else to look." Her voice a little sharp at the end. More for herself and the situation.

But she realized what it could sound like and took a deep breath. "Thank you, Gordon, for finding Charlotte's birth certificate. You are a marvel of efficiency. But it seems to be a blind lead. There is no one at the hotel with a surname anything like Blignaut at all and I will be careful not to get in the way of your investigation. I am only concerned with helping you figure out who did it."

She shook her head and continued. "I was so sure Charlotte's mother was the answer to all our questions. I haven't told you this before, but I do have an ability to dream dreams, revealing secrets. And the secret told to me by Charlotte in my dreams is this whole murder revolves around things about her mother and parentage."

He opened a picnic basket and offered her a sandwich. He must have stopped at the hotel first as they were tiny with the crusts cut off.

He took a sandwich of his own as he mused over her words. "Mmm well Shakespeare said 'there are more things in heaven and earth than can be dreamed of in your philosophy.' And who am I to argue with the bard? I saw things in the war unexplained in anyone's philosophy especially mine. So, you dream dreams. Well I had better hope your dreams of me will always be happy ones."

Helen watched his reaction. Even though she had known him for years she hadn't told him or even

David about her ability. She had always been afraid someone would mock her. "Gordon, aren't you surprised I have these weird dreams? You seem very accepting of it and I really thought you would think I was a bit doo lally."

"Doo lally? No. I saw so many strange things in the war and I no longer doubt there are forces at work unseen and unexplained. And I trust you Helen, you are sensible and sane. Why would I doubt what you tell me?" Gordon smiled at her and lifted his hand to gently touch her cheek.

Helen held her breath as his fingers lightly brushed against her skin. His hand dropped. "Let's not talk about depressing things like murder mysteries. When I got back to Pietermaritzburg it felt empty without you there. What I really want to say is you are looking beautiful today."

Gordon pulled her nearer with his hand. His eyes drew her in. "The kiss you gave me the other day has been keeping me awake at night and I think we need to explore it a bit more."

"Stop talking so much Gordon," Helen whispered. She pushed him back onto the blanket and leaned down to run her lips softly over his.

"Oh, heck no, girl. This is one area you will not take charge." His voice edged with amusement. Rolling her over he bent down to nibble her bottom lip. She felt her breath catch in her throat as she closed her eyes in anticipation of his passionate kisses. She could feel his breath on her face when suddenly a call came out from the road.

"What have we here? Young lovers in the wild." Mary laughingly popped her head through the leaves as Helen blushed from her toes to her nose. "Sorry, I shouldn't have intruded, but I was just on my Sunday stroll and I saw a flash of something intriguing and couldn't help myself. I haven't met this young man yet, but I am sure it could be no one else but the constable Fiona has been raving over."

Gordon jumped up and said, "Yes, guilty as charged. I am Gordon Brown and who might you be fair lady?"

Helen had no choice but to introduce Mary to Gordon and stand for a moment talking about inane things to pass the time. Common courtesy demanded they should at least make a comment about the weather and a few other unimportant things before they could make their farewells.

"Great weather we are having. It's a nice day for a walk and Gordon has driven up from Pietermaritzburg for the day," Helen commented hoping the bland conversation would give Mary a hint.

"Yes, it is good weather for a walk as well as other outdoor pursuits." Mary winked at them both and then said, "Well toodle-doo, I had better be going. I have guests to feed and entertain. Nice to see you again Helen and I can certainly see what Fiona means about you Gordon. Helen is a lucky girl." Mary walked off and left Gordon looking sheepishly at Helen. He carefully dusted down Helen's skirt so no grass or leaves stuck to her.

"Hop back on the bike and we will get to the hotel." He didn't mention the kiss and started packing up the things he had brought.

Chapter Twenty-Eight

Feeling suddenly all alone, Helen took a deep breath and turned away from the glade where she had hoped for more intimacy but where she felt dismissed as nothing more than a thrill for the moment. She climbed onto the motor bike.

Helen leaned her head against Gordon's back as they bumped along the road. The journey was much too short for her liking. She felt herself flush as she remembered Gordon's hands brushing her down and the gentle way he had placed the jacket around her shoulders.

She remembered the sensation of the kiss and its promise of more to come. A warmth seemed to spread from the centre of her being as she allowed her imagination to run riot. Gordon whistled against the wind.

The others were still at lunch and though they had already eaten some sandwiches it had been far too little. So they both sat down to lunch. Afterwards Helen took Wisp for a walk in the gardens. Helen took her sketch pad with them. Gordon lay on the lawn and was soon snoring softly as Helen tried to remember all Perla had taught them about watching the negative space in their drawings as she sketched a section of garden.

Ada joined her with her own pencil and sketchpad and as they drew, they chatted quietly so as not to wake Gordon. "Maisie seemed pleased to be remembered by Perla. Just imagine the two of them as young mothers in Durban during the Great War? How old would they have been? Perla said she was born in 1888, making them twenty something year olds during the war. Thirty by the end of the war. And so many responsibilities placed on their young shoulders." Helen held her drawing out at arm's length and squinted her eyes to focus on the basic shapes.

"Mom, remember what Fiona said about Charlotte's mother? She was a mother with two young boys when she had an affair and Charlotte had been the result. Could it be possible Maisie is Charlotte's mother?" Gordon grunted as he sat up.

"What are you two talking about? Not Charlotte again. I thought we agreed you would leave it up to me and anyhow the name on the birth certificate says Cornelia, not Maisie. No proof of any connection between the two." Gordon sat up and smiled indulgently at Helen. "But I suppose I can get one of the office staff to look for a marriage certificate for the major and Maisie. Shouldn't be too difficult with a surname like Swindells-Smythe. Can't be too many of them in the archives. Might as well cover all the bases."

"What a strange saying. Where did you get the reference to bases?" Helen smiled at Gordon as he stood up and towered over them.

Reaching out his hand to help them up, he laughed. "Just one of the things the Yanks taught us in the war. Some reference to baseball I think. They tried to get a game going every chance they could and it was actually quite good fun. Good way to blow off steam between all the bombs and deaths." His eyes clouded over probably thinking of David like she was.

"Sorry Helen, sometimes I forget how awful the war really was."

Both of them stood for a moment remembered David and his senseless death. Ada piped up. "David would not want either of you standing here moping away. He was full of the joys of life, singing and laughing every moment he could. Yes, he died too young and yes, we have a right to feel sadness, but let us look at the legacy of joy he brought into our lives. I think I can smell some fresh scones and cream and I for one think this fresh air is making me hungry. How on earth I am not the size of a house, I just don't know? Roast everything for lunch two hours ago and I am already famished." She picked up Wisp, who seemed happy to forgo the exercise, and Ada strode determinedly towards the hotel.

Ada called over her shoulder. "Helen, tomorrow we are climbing Amahaqwa Mountain, come hell or high water. I need to shake off this lethargy and get the blood pumping around my body again. Ancient rock paintings and great scenery will just be the cherry on the top."

Helen and Gordon looked at each other, pleased to finally be alone again. He put his arm around Helen and led her away from the hotel. Finding a quiet spot, he kissed her deeply, savouring every moment. "I have to go back home, Sweetheart. I shouldn't have driven up here today at all. But I had to see you and make sure you were safe and keeping out of trouble. Please promise me you won't do anything silly. I couldn't bear it if any harm came to you."

All Helen's doubts about how Gordon felt about her melted in the heat of his kiss. Helen nodded her

head in agreement to his request and hand in hand
they went in search of refreshment for Gordon.

Chapter Twenty-Nine

Gordon left soon after drinking a cup of tea and consuming a few delicate petit fours. Still licking his fingers, he jumped on his motorbike and roared off into the afternoon.

His day off work well spent with people he loved. He whistled as he negotiated the dusty road all the way back to the city, barely noticing the cattle wandering across the road, the goats appearing as if by magic and the multitude of little Zulu children demanding his attention.

He would stop for a moment, sip his water from his tin container, hand out treats to the children or shoo recalcitrant livestock from his path. His smile spread wider and wider as he remembered the day with Helen. The three-hour trip was filled with dreams and memories that had him longing for each moment of every day to be spent with his love.

Gordon rounded a corner only to be confronted with a large herd of cattle all mooing and shifting around. The young herd boys were dashing left and right with knobkerries raised and voices calling in a desperate effort to shift the beasts along. Gordon switched off his bike and stretched his back by raising his arms high above his head.

"Ama Baas I see you." Gordon looked down into the rheumy eyes of an ancient Zulu lady who had appeared through the dust and the noise as if by magic. "I'm Gogo. The ancestors have whispered that you are on important business Baas. Not the business of finding a killer but the business that will affect many generations ahead."

Gordon shook his head as he considered what the old lady had said. "Gogo I see you. You are indeed a wise and clever lady but I think the ancestors are talking about someone else. We have never met and yes, I'm on duty to find a killer but it is important. Finding murderers is always of prime interest to me and my seniors. I cannot think of what could be more important than that?"

"Aaah Indoda ebukekayo. Handsome man with no idea what life is all about. There are more pressing issues than chasing after something that the spirits can solve without the interference of humans. Remember that families are eternal and that your ancestors are busy working on finding you happiness. And now the cows are gone and you are informed of your true purpose. Hamba gahle, go well Indoda. Go well."

Gordon looked up to see the road ahead of him clear of all the beasts and young men. He turned to say goodbye to Gogo, only to find that the road behind him was also devoid of life.

"Oh well that was strange. Vanishing grandmothers and herds of cattle that turn into evening mist. Let's hope I can get home safely after the strangest but best day for a long time."

Whistling tunelessly Gordon started up his bike and completed his journey with no more odd occurrences at all and he was able to return to his contemplation of more pleasant pursuits with Helen.

Chapter Thirty

Back at the hotel, Ada and Helen sat in the lounge working on their sketches and Maisie joined them to chat about their experience with Perla.

"Wasn't Perla amazing recognising me after all these years? I must have been twenty-five or six when we last met and here we are all these years later? One of her sons died in the war. Very sad. She had two boys and a girl. Lovely children. I never visited them at home, but we would meet at different activities put on for the wives of servicemen. She has hardly changed a bit. I would have recognised her in a moment of course."

Maisie gushed. "I am so fortunate that neither of my sons went to war. One suffers from flat feet and the other from a heart murmur. Not that I would wish bad health on my boys but it certainly was a relief when they found jobs at home safe from bombs and bullets. The major was stationed in Cyprus for a while and later in London. He thoroughly enjoys the excitement of war but he too was pleased that his sons didn't follow in his footsteps. World War two will hopefully see the end of all this senseless killing for power but I doubt it."

Maisie regaled them with stories of hardship suffered by the women. Bemoaning the loneliness of waiting to hear of the fate of their loved ones so far away. Children growing up without a father and of youth fading too fast. She cried to think of all those who died during the Spanish flu epidemic. Lost in her own little world, she divulged much of her life. Helen were fascinated at this glimpse of a bye-gone era.

"Nothing was the same after the Great war. Gerald stayed in the army of course and we moved often. He was promoted and given different assignments. China, India, Australia for a while and some of the African countries too. Kenya was my favourite spot. We have lived all over the world and it's only now he is retired we have a chance to settle down and create a home of our own," Maisie said quietly.

Coming out of her reverie, she suddenly looked at Ada and said, "What is your story? Did your man go to the Great war?"

Ada nodded her head. "Yes, but he was injured quite early on. In the Somme, in July 1916. He was sent home and studied to be a doctor. A bullet in the leg was no barrier to his ability to heal and care for the sick. He always wanted to help people around him. The war did change him, but he was at peace with not taking a more active part in it."

Helen missed her father as she listened to her mother speak of his life. "The Spanish flu was devastating for him. He himself contracted the flu and it weakened his heart. He died aged only fifty-five and I miss his presence every day. I have two sons and three daughters. I was blessed to have them around me to support me through the dark days of life."

Ada patted Helen on the arm and brushed a tear away from her eyes. "Neither of my sons went to World War Two. They were working at supplying the war effort from here in South Africa. The skills they learned have stood them in good stead for their own businesses. Both of them set up general dealerships in Pietermaritzburg. Helen here has been helping their two wives keep the home fires and the stores burning while they were elsewhere. I do wish one of them had become a doctor like their father but they are happy doing what they do." Helen didn't want to burst her mother's bubble by telling her that she wouldn't be working for her brothers any more.

The major arrived and Maisie went off for a walk with her husband. There were people spread-eagled over the furniture in the lounge and Ada and Helen soon retired to their rooms to read their books.

CHAPTER THIRTY-ONE

Wisp cuddled up on Helen's lap, the sun throwing sun beams across the floor of the room and the air was cosy and warm. The book slipped from Helen's fingers but she hardly noticed as the fingers of sleep tickled her mind.

She saw her old friend, the burning man, standing at the window. He had a smile on his face for once and was not calling for help. Charlotte was perched on a chair at the window and turned to look at Helen. "Well are you my friend or not?" She asked.

"Charlotte, of course I'm your friend. I need to find out why you were killed and then I can find the evidence to tie the murderer to the crime. I cannot just point a finger and be believed. What happened?" Helen replied.

"Oh, well, I asked my mother for money. You know I deserve it, don't you? And she said no. I had the knobkerrie in my hand and must have put it down. I took it along to make sure she knew I was serious. I borrowed the fighting stick from Mr. van Rooyen's office. He never uses it except for decoration and I didn't think he would miss it. My Mom suddenly went all strange and fell over."

Charlotte's ghost seemed a little restless as she smoothed a hand over her skirt. "I think she fainted. I wanted to help her. I really didn't want to hurt her except emotionally. But then I was hit. Hard. I looked down to see where the knobkerrie was and it was gone. All I saw was a pair of man's shoes. And the world went black."

She looked up with surprise written all over her face. "My Mom didn't do it. Oh Helen, my Mom didn't kill me." Tears ran down her cheeks as she gently touched the back of her head. "I thought she had done it. I really did."

Charlotte faded into the mists of twilight and Helen stirred to find Wisp gently kneading her stomach and sucking on her dress.

"Oh Wisp, now I will have to change clothes. Right you are my girl, no walk for you this evening." Wisp flipped over onto her back and presented her tummy to be tickled. "Silly girl, you know just how to get me to change my mind." Helen laughed at her feline's ability to charm her mistress.

Her mind went over the revelations Charlotte had talked about as she changed her dress. Charlotte having supplied her own murder weapon was a shock. But the fact it was a man who had attacked her was no real surprise.

It would have taken someone with strength to move Charlotte to the top of the stairs and she shivered as she remembered her close call the night before in Charlotte's bedroom. Definitely a man. Could it be the major? He had seemed too drunk to wield a weapon the last time Helen had seen him, and yet he was a man trained in combat. Perhaps he had come to the protection of his wife? But he had no motive really.

A sharp word would most probably have been enough to stop the altercation, why kill her? Why throw Charlotte down the stairs? The more information Helen received, the more confusing it all became. The major did not resemble the man in the bedroom and Helen decided to eliminate him from her list of suspects. Of course, there was no actual list and if there had been there would have been no names on the list at all.

Time to have a heart to heart with Maisie. A little bit of truth would not hurt the situation. In fact, a whole lot of truth would be best Helen thought as she combed her hair and got ready to go downstairs.

Chapter Thirty-Two

The Swindells-Smythe couple sat outside sipping on sundowners when Helen approached with her mother. The major lifted his glass to them and said, "Two more beautiful ladies come to join an ugly old man. How fortunate for me. A thorn between the roses. What can I get for you? A shandy like Maisie is drinking or a wine?"

He looked like he had been imbibing in more than just a shandy or two and was gaily waving his drink around until it splashed out over the flagstones. The Marashino cherry looked like a ship tossed on a storm troubled sea as the drink swished from side to side.

"Aah Major Swindells-Smythe a glass of wine mixed with a touch of soda will suit us. Many thanks for the invite and the compliment. What a splendid evening it is. The sunset is superb. Look at the colour of those clouds. Wow, I don't think I have ever seen such a vibrant sight. We are very fortunate to be enjoying this all aren't we? Good company, great view and a fantastic setting. Perfect." Helen gushed as Ada sat down next to Maisie and Helen took the seat on the far side of the small table.

The conversation ranged from good food to the effects of the shortage of men in the workforce after the war. The major was quite outspoken about where a woman's place should be. "I know the ladies have been doing stellar work to keep the home fires burning while we men were off fighting the enemies of freedom. But the men are home now, and it is time for life to return to normal. Men at work and women at home." He twirled his moustache and peered at the women around him as if challenging them to argue.

Maisie sat up straight and looked her husband in his eye. "Poppycock Gerald. Women are quite capable of looking after themselves and their families while holding down a demanding job. While you have been swanning off on the battlefields of the world acting the hero, the women have been home being true heroines. It's the day to day grind we battle. Often with no support from the men in our lives."

Maisie wiped a tear from her eye as she stared down her blustering husband. "I am not saying what you did was worth nothing, but then neither is what we women did either," Maisie declared vehemently.

Helen was quite shocked at the change in this woman who had seemed like a quiet little mouse when they first arrived. Maisie had found a backbone and developed quite a character over the past few days. The Major was not looking happy at his wife's sudden change of demeanour.

"Gerald you are being insulting. What is young Helen supposed to do with her life? Sit around all her life waiting for some man to rescue her? Well what happens if the men are not available? I would love for the world to be normal as you call it, but sadly it will never return to what it used to be. And maybe it shouldn't. Gerald, I love you very much, but sometimes you say things and you don't make any sense at all." Maisie smiled at her husband, but Helen noticed Maisie's hand shook slightly as she took up her glass again.

The mouse had turned into a lion, but the mouse was still inside Maisie quivering with fear. "Thank you, Maisie, for defending me. Major I know men want us to be just like their mothers and grandmothers since time immemorial, but Hilter changed our expectations. We can't go back to being so dependent on our men. It's not fair on them and it's not fair to limit women who have enjoyed earning their own money. If all our men were like you, then maybe the world would be a better place but unfortunately good men went away to war and some of them never came back," Helen said sadly.

After this exchange the Major decided he would rather drink with the men at the bar and left the women to their conversations. This suited Helen down to the ground.

The major leaned down and gave his wife a peck on her cheek. "I will be back to walk you in to dinner dear." Maisie smiled up at him and patted his hand before he turned and made his way down the stairs.

Taking a small sip of her wine spritzer, Helen turned to Maisie and said, "Tell me, where did you get such a lovely name? I don't know many Maisies. Is it a British name?"

Maisie laughed and said, "Well, actually my real name is Cornelia. My Mom was Afrikaans and all her family have these long Afrikaans names. None of the family had short names. Oupa Blignaut was Johannes Jacobus Hermanus Daniel. Everyone called him JJ for short.' Maisie lifted her drink up in silent toast to her long dead ancestors. 'Mom's first husband was a Mr. Cooper and my half-sister is Margareta, or was, as she has recently passed away. Named for her grandmother. I will not bore you with what her full name was. Just know she complained bitterly every time she had to fill in a form."

Musa hovered close and Maisie close to ask if there might be some snacks to have with the drinks. He went off to see what could be found and Maisie continued her monologue of memories. 'Her Dad, my Mom's first husband, died of some lung disease when Margareta was just a few days old. Then Mom married my Dad and when I was born they named me Cornelia, but Margareta called me Meisie, it is the Afrikaans word for girl. She found the name Cornelia too much to say.'

Musa arrived with a tray of small sandwiches and sausage meat encased in pastry that had Helen's mouthwatering at the aroma. Helen and Ada both helped themselves and Maisie sighed deeply as she considered her words.

"When I met Gerald, he misheard my name and called me Maisie. The name stuck and now it's only a few cousins who call me Cornelia or Meisie. I don't mind at all. A new life with Gerald and a new name seemed quite romantic at the time."

Maisie got a dreamy look on her face as she thought of her family. "I named my sons very simple names. I was not popular with the family for not following the traditions, but I thought there was too many Johannes Jacobus boys to carry on the tradition. I named them Daniel and Herman, so not too far from tradition." She laughed.

Helen was loath to break the good mood but she might never get such a great opportunity again to find out the truth. Gordon might think she was getting into dangerous waters but Helen had a good feeling about Maisie. Leaning forward Helen said quietly, "Maisie you know we have been helping the constable with his investigations? Talking to others who might know what happened. Maisie, I don't want to shock you but we know you were with Charlotte when she was killed. Can you tell us what you saw? Oh dear, don't faint on us now my dear. Here, have a sip of your shandy." Helen quickly tipped the jug of ice into a cloth and applied it to the base of Maisie's neck.

Ada patted Maisie hand and Helen quietly continued talking, "We also know Charlotte was your daughter and she was threatening to extort money from you. But we also believe it was not you who killed her. It was a man. Did you see anything?"

Maisie took a deep breath and a large gulp of her drink. "I thought I had kept it a secret. Even Gerald doesn't know about my daughter. She was the result of an indiscretion during the Great War. I never wanted to hurt anyone, but I was so alone and I am sorry but all I can say was I was young and silly."

The tears were running down her cheeks as she continued. "Margareta said she would bring her up as her own, and I knew she would love Charlotte as if she were her child." She emptied her glass and Helen called over the waiter to order another beer shandy.

"A little bit more beer and a little less lemonade this time Sipho. Thank you," Helen instructed the waiter.

They could hear Gerald laughing with the men in the pub and after their glasses had been refilled by a waiter, Maisie continued on. "Gerald held the purse strings very tight and I couldn't send them any money, but I sent a large hamper each Christmas. Gerald was happy for me to send gifts for my only sister. I dare not write letters or send cards just in case Gerald found them and my secret would be out. Once the boys were grown, I did manage to send a bit more help to Margareta.”

She wiped her eyes with a lacy handkerchief. “For a while Charlotte even went to St Cuthbert’s school for girls. Then Margareta got ill and couldn’t work to pay the bills. My little contribution was not enough to pay for the boarding school and Charlotte left school to work to help support he aunt.”

“Then Margareta died and I decided to come and speak to Charlotte. I told Gerald I wanted to come to the mountains for the fresh air and he was happy to oblige. But Charlotte was angry. Very angry. She threatened to tell Gerald and wanted money to compensate for all the years of want. The last night, she was standing over me with the knobkerrie raised, when I started to faint, she put the stick against the wall and the last thing I remember was a shadow coming up behind her. When I heard the next day she had died, I was shaken to the core. All I remember of the night Charlotte was killed was I had come around from my faint lying on the floor of the passage. Charlotte’s bedroom door was closed and I thought she had just left me lying there on my own. But the poor girl was lying at the bottom of the stairs. My poor little girl thought I didn’t love her. And now I can’t tell her.” She sobbed and sobbed.

Helen gently wiped the tears from Maisie’s eyes with a wet cloth and Ada had her arm around the distraught woman in comfort. “There, there Maisie. Don’t distress yourself. You did your best to give her a good home. She will be looking down now and know you love her. Come now, let’s get you looking your beautiful self before your husband returns.”

Helen waited until Maisie had herself under control before asking her if she remembered anything more about the shadowy man on the landing. "Close your eyes Maisie and picture the night. What colour was his shirt? And was he wearing a particular type of shoes? Anything you can tell us will help Gordon with the investigation. A smell, an impression, anything could help find out who it was."

Maisie obligingly closed her eyes and for a moment she sat quietly before sitting up and said, "Blue shirt. I remember a blue shirt. Shoes? I think they were those work boots the men at the jail wear. Not shiny. I think they were brown leather."

She smiled for the first time since they had started their interrogation. "Do you think this will help you find out who did this to my baby?"

"Oh, absolutely. Invaluable. Now we need to remember which man was wearing a blue shirt on the night. It can't be too difficult surely?" Helen spent a moment trying to picture all the men in the pub the night Charlotte had died.

Steve had been wearing a striped blue shirt and Sam had on an old khaki shirt but could it have been Steve? Helen remembered the shirt as being very pale and not immediately noticeably blue. The major crossed the patio towards them and Helen thanked Maisie for her honesty. Helen went in to dinner with her Mom. Ada had to kick her under the dinner table once or twice when people spoke to her and she was far away in her thoughts and didn't answer respond.

Chapter Thirty-Three

Finally, Helen took Wisp for a walk before retiring. Her head pounded with a headache starting just behind her eyes and she was craving fresh air and peace. Fiona and Ruth both suggested she might be pining for a certain young constable and Sue had offered the contents of her medicine chest in case it was something medical or serious.

Helen shrugged off the teasing and the offer of drugs before going upstairs to collect her cat. The two of them took a slow walk through the gardens as night fell softly around them. Wisp rubbed herself against Helen's legs as they stopped to smell a particular rose.

Ada called from the veranda to say they had an early morning and it was time they were both tucked up in bed. Helen and Wisp turned away from the night shrouded flowers and followed the light of the hotel to find their way to their beds.

No ghosts came to disturb their sleep and it was only as the light of dawn crept over the countryside Helen felt sleep slipping away as sunlight touched her eyelids.

She dressed in her sensible clothes for the hike and put a canvas backpack on her back to contain the drawing supplies, her camera and her cat. Wisp was happy to snuggle down in her special carrier for a day out in the wilds.

Ada's backpack contained a bottle of chilled water and a snack packed for them by an obliging Musa. Fiona waved to them as they strode off up the path.

"It's quite beautiful up there. I am not offering to accompany you, once was enough for me. Enjoy yourselves," Fiona called as she smoothed down a brightly coloured pencil skirt.

Ruth sat at a table under the trees preparing her lesson for the day and laying out books and pencil in anticipation of her student joining her. She too waved them off happily before returning to her preparations.

Everyone else had gone off to work and the women looked up at the Amahaqwa peeping out of a haze. The mist burned off before they reached the steep part of the hike and they knew it would be another hot day.

A snake lazed on a rock and slithered off as they approached. A baboon barked a warning at them and Helen called out, "Good morning Mr. Baboon. No need to fear us. We are but visitors to your world." A family of Hyraxes skittered away and even a small Duiker came out of the underbrush to greet them. Helen took photos of the animals and the abundance of flowers peeping out between rocks and grass.

The women did not push themselves to climb quickly, but rather they took it slow and enjoyed the experience of being at one with nature. Ada needed to take a breather along the way and Helen was happy to join her in her slow ascent.

They finally reached the cave with the ancient rock paintings. Taking out the water and snacks, they set up their picnic on a large rock and surveyed the countryside. Far away to the East a faint blue marked the sea and to the North and South the mighty Drakensberg Mountains towered above them.

Helen undid the backpack to let the cat out of the bag. Wisp happily scratched in the dirt for a moment and then sat on the large rock to observe her domain. Secure in her superiority, she relaxed in the warm sunlight.

Helen photographed the rock paintings and then took a photo of her mother and Wisp looking over the valley below them. As Ada lay back in the sun, Helen did some quick sketches of the rock paintings.

She wondered about the ancient artist's hand who had created this amazing art work and what their lives had been like. Their challenges would be all about hunting and finding shelter for their families. She remembered the ghostly figures she had seen in the glade and felt the presence of the ancient artist looking down at her. How simple a bye gone time seemed in this post war era.

She thought of Maisie and her life of secrecy. Hiding from her husband such a vital part of her life. A child should never be forgotten or made to feel unimportant. She understood Charlotte's anger as well as Maisie's internal battle.

So, if it wasn't a family affair, what could have caused someone to murder a young woman? Love? Lust? Jealousy? And who could have these feelings? Helen listed the men at the hotel on the back of her drawing book.

Steve, married lover. No, he seemed genuinely surprised at Charlotte being murdered.

Sam, was he a jilted or spurned lover jealous of Steve and Charlotte. No, he seemed to be more than happy with the girls of the district to test out his charms on.

Johan of the cheeky smile and charming ways didn't seem like someone able to kill for love. He would just move on to the next conquest.

Gert was a quiet man keeping much to himself and it didn't seem like he had ever even spoken to Charlotte. He kept to himself except when working or drinking at the pub. The suspect list was back to nil and not a clue in sight.

Helen carefully packed all their things back into the backpacks as she went through the list of hotel guests in her mind.

Suddenly she stopped in her tracks. What if the murderer thought Maisie could identify him? Was Maisie at risk? A cold shiver went down Helen's back as she realised the possibilities they had not thought of.

"Mom, we missed something. What if the murderer thinks Maisie can identify him? Her life could be in danger. Come, there is not a moment to be lost. We need to find the man in the shadows." Picking Wisp up and sliding the cat into the backpack took a moment and by this time Ada was standing up and dusting herself off. Wisp looked disgusted at this invasion of her enjoyment, but soon settled down in the nice warm confines of the backpack and could be heard purring as Helen shucked the bag onto her back.

"Helen, surely he would have tried something before this. He has had a few days to plan something. And anyhow, Maisie is always in company. Either her husband or the other guests. There wouldn't be a moment he could do his dastardly deed without being observed. But maybe we should warn her not to take chances?"

Ada shrugged herself into the straps of the backpack and picking up her walking stick, she strode off down the mountain and back toward the hotel. No need to rest on the way down, Ada seemed energized and happily kept up a blistering pace pushing Helen to keep up with her much older mother.

CHAPTER THIRTY-FOUR

Reaching the bottom of the valley in a significantly shorter time than it had taken them to climb it, they approached the hotel. Pamela was at the reception desk and Helen breathlessly asked whether she had seen Maisie. "Oh no, her and the Major had a bit of a spat at breakfast and she said she needed some fresh air. She has been gone for a while now. She said she might go and visit Mary across the road. She should be back anytime soon. Lunch is almost ready and she never misses her meals."

"Can you phone Mary and see whether Maisie is still there? I really need to speak to her." Helen managed not to sound paranoid as she pressed Pamela to make the phone call.

"Okay. But I am sure she will be walking through those doors any moment now." She dialed the switchboard and was soon being connected to Mary. "Ah Mary, this is Pamela Meaker from the Mountain Park Hotel. Do you think you could tell me if Mrs. Swindells-Smythe is still with you? She left soon after breakfast and we are becoming concerned she has not returned yet." Pamela asked into the phone.

"Well Fiona is here, but neither she nor I have seen hide nor hair of Mrs. Swindells-Smythe. She didn't get here at all. Maybe she changed her mind. Or else she might have had an accident and be somewhere along the path. But she is definitely not with me." Mary sounded concerned as she answered.

Helen took off her backpack, much to the dismay of Wisp who let out a hiss at her mistress. "We will go and look for her. I'm sure we will find her safe and sound and bring her back to eat her lunch in no time at all." Helen announced to a concerned looking Pamela.

"If you could get Delphinia to take our bags up to our rooms, we would be very appreciative. Thank you."

Still carrying her walking stick, Ada followed her daughter through the doors and at a fast trot, took off down the road towards Mary's boarding house. Wisp had jumped onto Helen's shoulders and was now perched imperiously as her mistress walked down the road.

There was a section of gorse encroaching upon the path, but otherwise there was no place of concealment. A few places where there was a ditch she might have fallen into, but none of them revealed an injured or distressed Maisie. Fiona and Mary met them at the halfway point saying they too had seen no sign of the lady in question. Helen suggested they all take their time along the path looking for any sign of struggle and work their way back to their starting points.

"We are looking to see if Maisie might have slipped and fallen somewhere. Or maybe a struggle of some sort," Helen said quietly.

Mary gave them a strange look at the mention of a struggle but complied with the suggestion. "I will walk back toward the boarding house and I'll phone the hotel if I find Maisie and you do the same from your side. Phone me if you find her."

They walked slowly back to where they had started their search and found nothing unexpected. Wisp hissed as branches brushed against Helen's shoulder and threatened to knock her off her mount. Helen grabbed her mother's walking stick to push aside grasses and the gorse, to no avail.

Standing at the bottom of the driveway to the hotel, Helen stopped and cast her eyes over the pathway. She stroked Wisp distractedly as she looked around.

"Nothing Mom, not a single sign of what might have happened to Maisie. I'm worried about her," Helen admitted.

Pamela and Mr. van Rooyen were standing on the front doorstep waiting to see what they had discovered. Helen shook her head and Mr. van Rooyen sighed deeply as he went inside to organise a proper search. First a murder and now a disappearance. This was not good for the hotel or business.

CHAPTER THIRTY-FIVE

Helen went in search of the major, but Mr. van Rooyen had beaten her to the table where Maisie's husband sat.

The major scowled at his bowl of soup when Mr. van Rooyen bent down and whispered the fact his wife was missing.

"What? Speak up man. Did you say my Maisie is missing? Well go and find her. I'm sure she is sitting sulking somewhere. Send out the Zulu staff immediately. They will know where to look." He put down his spoon and stood up and glared around at the few people in the dining room.

"Have any of your people seen my wife? She seems to have disappeared. Very inconvenient. Spoiling our lunch with her dramatics. Silly woman."

Mrs. van Rooyen said, "I saw Maisie from my bedroom window walking towards the road, but she seemed fine. I didn't think anything of it. It's a lovely day out and I envied her being able to go out for a walk."

Sue said, "I saw Maisie crossing the highway and thought it strange the Major had not been with her but I was busy and did not stop to ask her why. She seemed fine."

Steve said, "I will drive over to the building site and find out if she has perhaps wandered as far as the jail. Some of the guys have been out and about collecting supplies and they might have seen something." Picking up his jacket he strode out and climbed into his work truck.

As if he could sense the drama was about to unfold, Gordon drove up on his motorbike. Helen rushed over to him as he walked into the hotel. "Gordon, thank goodness you are here. Maisie is missing and we are just about to mount a search." Gordon put his arm around Helen and gave her a quick hug.

"The boss sent me back to collect the last of Charlotte's effects and to see if I could get any more information. But I can certainly help in any way I can." Gordon turned to Mr. van Rooyen with his offer of assistance.

Helen waited to see if the major would organise a proper search, but he seemed at a loss. He mumbled, "It was just a silly argument. Silly woman hysterics."

Mr. van Rooyen called all the staff together and told them to search the hotel grounds and in each room. "Make sure there is nowhere she could be hidden. Every room needs to be searched. Do you understand? Good. I expect you back here in about an hour. Pamela if you could assign an area of the grounds to half the staff and the hotel to the other half, it would be a great help."

Pamela raised her voice and started giving out assignments, "Delphinia, Alphina and Seraphina you take the top floor." Like a sergeant major she organised her troops and soon they were all gainfully employed in the search.

She told them what clothes Maisie wore and even what type of shoes she wore. Helen smiled as she thought of Pamela working with Winston Churchill. It would have been a sight to see. Petite Pamela with her deceptively gentle voice had transformed into a giant of a warrior in the space of a few minutes. Another mouse into a lioness transformation.

Chapter Thirty-Six

The day dragged on for what seemed like eons, while teams came in with reports of empty rooms and secluded glades empty of life. Steve and his workers had downed tools to look for Maisie. Sam's usual bonhomie was dimmed and he didn't joke or laugh as they searched in ditches and under bushes.

At five o'clock Musa came in holding a shoe. Pamela identified it as having belonged to Maisie and the search was concentrated to the area of the find. It had been found in the orchard of the neighbouring property far away from where they had been looking. Musa said there was a drag mark going into the bush.

The major insisted on joining the search and huffing and puffing, he dashed off down the path and through the shallow stream. Hands helped him up the other side of the river bank and finally he stood under a spreading apple tree looking at the spot his wife had struggled with an unknown attacker and where he shoe had marked the activity.

The major's face crumpled. Helen watched in sympathy. Maisie could be dead or severely injured by a madman. The drag marks were plain to see and Steve and Sam were the first down the track in pursuit of the kidnapper.

Helen heard a scream and increased her speed. The major had dropped to the ground, but when the scream split the air, he was on his feet in an instant. "Maisie, sweetheart, I forgive you. I'm coming to save you."

Helen was no match for the dense bush and soon it was the younger men who once again took the lead. The Zulu men had taken a different tack and were silently working their way through the bush in a pincer movement. If they could come at the kidnapper from behind or from the sides, they might be able to surprise him. They communicated with odd whistles seeming to bounce off the sides of the mountain above them.

Johan and some of the men went left and others up the hill in search of the elusive victim and her captor. Helen, Gordon, Ada and the major stayed on a vague game track, holding onto each other as they struggled through the path.

They could hear the rest of the searchers ranging far and wide. The major collapsed onto a rock and could go no further.

"Major, have you noticed anyone suspicious looking around here lately. I think she must have known her attacker because, surely, she would have screamed before now." Gordon queried.

Helen leaned down to offer the major a sip of water from her water bottle but he shook his head and said, "I have a flask of my own."

Taking it out of his pocket he took a deep drink of the liquid. He looked dejected and beaten as Gordon sat down next to him. "We will find her Major, never fear."

Helen had a strange feeling pulling her down the path and she informed Ada she would go with Gordon. "We won't go far Mom, we will leave you to find out what you can from the major without our presence to cramp your style," Helen assured her.

Helen left Ada to deal with the major and quietly continued on. Looking carefully at where she was stepping. The tug inside of her guided her steps. Gordon touched her hand and whispered. "Let me go first Helen. It's too dangerous for you and at least I know how to protect myself and you if needed."

"Oh Gordon, I am a big girl. You don't need to be my protector. I have a good feeling about this and don't feel scared of what we will find," Helen replied.

"Helen, I know you are capable of looking after yourself but I like being your knight in shining armour. Come on, let me go first so that I can the hero for once." He smiled as he said this and Helen stopped and looked back over her shoulder.

"You are my hero, Gordon. But this is something I need to do."

"Oh, what the heck. There will no doubt be times when I can actually be your great protector. Go ahead, I will have your back," Gordon answered.

In the hush after their whispered conversation they heard a soft sob. Helen stopped again and Gordon touched her shoulder in support. Another sob was followed by a harsh admonition to shut up.

"I'm trying to talk to you Maisie. Stop crying and just listen. Please shut up." The voice was masculine and Helen tried hard to recognise the person. She brushed aside a few grasses when suddenly the bush gave way to a clearing next to a shallow pool in the riverbed.

Standing in the water was Gert holding Maisie tightly with a knife pushed against her neck. "Don't come any closer. I can kill her in an instant," He hissed loudly enough to be heard by Helen but not by others further away.

Helen was shocked at the sight of the young man. "Gert, you can't mean this. She's innocent. Why are you doing this? Let her go. Be a good guy and just let Maisie go." She raised her voice slightly in the hope Ada and the searchers would hear her and come running but the surrounding bush absorbed her voice and even if she had raised her voice it would have bounced off the steep cliffs soaring above them.

Gert looked at Helen with eyes glazed over with anger. "I was trying to help her. She saw me this morning and I could see she remembered what had happened to Charlotte and what I had done. So, I waited until she was walking through the bush and I grabbed her. Just to talk with her. To try and explain why I had to kill Charlotte for all our sakes. I was out collecting nails from the stores and I didn't go looking for her but then I knew the fates had sent her to me. Charlotte was doing evil things. But Maisie wouldn't listen." Maisie wriggled in his arms and Gert put his hand across her mouth.

"I locked her in the downstairs bedroom all day. You know the one no one likes to go into. I thought she could think about what I had told her and she would be okay with what I had done. But then the alarm went out she was missing and I had to do something. She screamed and I brought her here. I thought we would have more time to talk, but then we heard you coming down the path."

Maisie wriggled in his arms and tears fell down her cheeks as she begged Gert to please let her go. "Gert, please, it need not be like this. Let me go. I have never hurt you and I loved Charlotte just like you did. She was my daughter."

Gert looked down at her and for a moment Helen thought he might release Maisie. "No. I can't let you go until you hear me. If she goes, then no one will know why I did what I did."

He looked around at Gordon before continuing. "I was Charlotte's dance partner before the war. I loved her and we were going to be married. Then I went to war and she started telling people I had left her for a Parisian woman. It was not true. I would never cheat on her. Not on Charlotte. She was the light of my life."

He stopped talking for a moment to adjust his grip on the knife. "I was in Egypt fighting for peace and a happy life back home with my darling and she was writing me letters making my heart ache. I don't have a way with words and I didn't know what to say to make her see how much I loved her."

Helen slowly eased herself into the water closer to Gert and Maisie. Gert did not notice the slow advance and continued on with the recitation of his woes his attention focused on Gordon. "I disembarked in Durban and went straight to Tongaat, but Charlotte was gone. It took me a few weeks to find out where she was and then I caught a train to Underberg. I walked from there to here. Two days I walked and what did she say when I finally arrived? She said she loved someone else. She said he was an honest and kind man, who had integrity. I got a job at the jail as a stone mason so I could be near her. And then I found out the man she was in love with was a man with no morals. No integrity."

Gert glared at Gordon. "Steve the foreman. Steve who spoke about his wife and children. Steve the cheater. He lied to her. Steve did. He used her. At the pub he said something cutting right to the core of who he is. A liar and a cheat."

Gert shook his head. Helen could see Gert's hand was shaking. "He said everyone found love outside of marriage sometime. And in a moment, I knew he was talking about my Charlotte. Pure love cannot be laid aside just because you are far away from home comforts. Steve said during the war he had many women who he loved. Maybe I should have killed him?"

Tears streamed down his cheeks as he cried for a lost love.

"I waited until we were all getting ready for bed and then I said I was going to the toilet. But I walked down to Charlotte's room to talk to her. To tell her I was the better man for her. What I found was her standing over Maisie with a knobkerrie raised above her head and demanding money. Suddenly the scales were off my eyes and I saw her for who she really was. A wrecker of dreams. She was prepared to hurt Steve's wife and children. She had killed my dreams of a loving wife and children and now she was threatening this kind lady." He looked down at Maisie and smiled.

Maisie shivered in his arms as he finished his story. "Maisie fainted and Charlotte put down the knobkerrie to lean forward and help her. I saw my moment and hit her on the back of the head with the discarded knobkerrie. She fell down and I thought I had just knocked her out. But I suppose I must have hit her harder than I thought. I wouldn't have killed her on purpose. I picked her up and carried her down the stairs to the next landing. I just wanted her to be away from Maisie. Somewhere she could no longer hurt others. The next morning, I heard she had had an accident and I was pleased."

Helen was now within reach of Gert and she held her breath in anticipation. A single glance in her direction and she could put herself and Maisie in danger.

"I didn't know Sue had been at the bottom of the stairs," Gert admitted.

He must have heard something because suddenly he swung around carrying Maisie with him. He looked at Gordon and pushed the knife into Maisie's neck until a small bead of blood dripped down onto her plain white blouse.

"Keep away from me. I'm not yet finished." Taking a step into deeper water he dragged his victim into the icy stream.

"I never expected her to be dead. She was the love of my life. She might have been doing evil, but I knew I could save her from herself. I hid the knobkerrie in my cupboard so she could not use it on anybody else. But then when I heard she was dead, I had to get rid of it. I threw it in the first bedroom I could find on my way out of the hotel in the morning."

His hands dropped to his sides and he pushed Maisie towards the bank and safety. Tears poured down his cheeks as he sobbed.

"My Charlotte, I'm sorry, so very sorry."

Still holding the knife in front of him to keep any pursuers at bay he stepped back until he teetered on the edge of the small waterfall. He took out a service pistol from his pocket and pointed it at Helen.

"Stay there. I don't want to hurt anyone else. I just want to rest. I want this all to go away. I'm sorry

Maisie you are a good lady and I wouldn't have hurt you. I was trying to save you."

Time moved slowly as Gert stepped backwards. His foot slipped on the rocks. His body tilted backwards his arms wind milling as he tumbled down into the white-water foaming and swirling at its base.

When Helen rushed forward to try and grab him, she saw a spreading pool of red amongst the pristine clear mountain stream. Gert had hit his head on a protruding rock and as they watched, his body floated down river.

Both the gun and the knife nowhere to be seen, his hands relaxed and finally at peace. His blue eyes wide open, unable to see the beauty around him or feel the hurt of a lost love as the light of life fluttered and died. A smile hovered around his mouth as he greeted someone on the other side of death's veil.

Helen stood staring over the waterfall in dismay, frozen to the spot. Gordon rushed to Helen's side and held her close to his breast as she shivered in shock.

They helped Maisie up the bank of the pool and Helen was just wrapping her arms around her when Ada and the major appeared through the bush. In seconds others joined them, Mr. van Rooyen called out to those further away. "We have found her. She is safe."

CHAPTER THIRTY-SEVEN

Strangely enough Maisie was the person least upset by the day's events. She hugged her husband and whispered, "Thank you for coming to look for me. I am sorry we argued. I have things to tell you that will explain why I have been so stressed lately. Come now. I need to change my clothes and then we can all have a stiff drink and try to forget the sadness of the day."

He put down his hot chocolate and followed her up the stairs like a puppy dog at its master's heel.

Glad that the kidnapping and attack hadn't upset Maisie Gordon turned to the more gruesome tasks of the day.

Gert's body was retrieved a mile down from the waterfall. His face untouched by the ravages of his journey. He had spoken enough with Gert to know his only living relative was a brother. He didn't look forward to explaining his brother's death. Gordon had already decided to leave out most of the story. It was not in anyone's favour to blacken his name when he was already in death's grasp.

Constable Gordon Brown and Doctor McTierney signed the death certificate as misadventure. The witnesses to this accidental death all said the same thing. Gert had been out looking for Maisie and gone to her aid only to slip on a rock and fall over the waterfall. Nothing anyone could do to save him.

Steve attested to Gert's great work ethic and how much he would be missed as a stonemason. Technically none of them were lying. They had not seen the final scene played out. Only the two women and Gordon had, and they were united in their silence.

Yes, Gert was a great worker and yes, he had tried to save Maisie. The death was an accident. No one pushed him, and no one could have saved him. Ada did ask if it was connected to the death of Charlotte. He couldn't bring himself to lie so he had answered vaguely, "We will never know now."

As to Maisie and her abduction. She said she had gone for a walk and got lost. Gert had found her and was helping her home when he had slipped and fallen. No one could get her to say any more. Even the major was at a loss as to why his wife would have wandered so far afield. He apologised for the argument causing Maisie to leave the hotel in such a distressed state.

"Maisie, sweetheart. I could not live without you by my side. When I thought you were lost to me I realised you are my breath and my heart," The Major admitted.

Maisie caught up his hands and smiled warmly at him. "Thank you, Gerald, it means the world to me to hear you say such sweet things. Let us go back to Margareta's house in Tongaat and start living the rest of our lives."

Chapter Thirty-Eight

Helen found Maisie alone at the cemetery where Pamela said she would be. Maisie sighed loudly when Helen trotted up with Wisp in her harness. Wisp stropped Maisie's legs and she crouched to give her a pat on the head. Helen asked, "Maisie are you alright."

Helen wasn't just asking about her feelings but about everything. About the secret they were keeping. Both her connection to Charlotte and how Gert had died.

"I am not without sin," She said softly. "I could have prevented this awful thing." Her eyes turned to the heavens as she said, "I wish you God's speed Gert and may you meet up with my daughter and remind her she is special." Maisie wrapped her arms around herself as she stood up and exited the chapel.

Helen caught a ghostly glimpse of Charlotte and Gert holding hands in the trees amongst the older gravestones but shook it off as a figment of her imagination. Both of them were damaged souls so maybe they had reunited in the spirit world. Who knew? Certainly not Maisie.

Helen took her by her hand for support. Then they wandered across the lawns and under the trees until they found another new grave. This one had flowers piled on top and a small marker saying, "Charlotte, beloved daughter of Cornelia and companion of her beloved aunt Margaretha. Born 12 November 1915 died 1 May 1946. Dance forever with the angels on the clouds of heaven sweet and lovely girl of my heart."

Maisie shed her tears of grief and then joined her new friends at a café. Over cups of tea they spoke of all they experienced over the past few days. Maisie admitted the difficult conversation she had with her husband. The major had been told of the relationship of Charlotte to his wife and Maisie had spoken of her years of secrecy. He had blustered and ranted until he had nothing more to say.

Maisie smiled, "He said he always wanted to be a chef and planned to enroll at a cordon bleu school at a local hotel. We will move into Margareta's small cottage. It won't be perfect but it is a change. A good change." Maisie confided to Helen.

"Gerald was shaken up when he thought he might lose me for good. I cannot condone what happened to Charlotte, but some good has come out of it all. I have my husband back. It's almost like we are newlyweds. He is losing his army attitude of command and obedience. He made his first meal last night and I thoroughly enjoyed every moment of it." Maisie admitted happily.

Helen smiled at her and finally told Maisie of how Charlotte had visited her dreams at the hotel. "She came to visit me one last time the final night we were there. Both she and Gert appeared. Gert wanted to say sorry for what he put you through. He says it was a moment of madness. He didn't think it through properly. He was aware he had crossed the line, but he wants you to know if he had survived he would have given himself in to the police for his punishment." Helen smiled at the image in her mind.

"Then Charlotte took his hand in my dream and they started dancing around the room. It was quite lovely. Charlotte had on a delicate white dress with high heels covered in lots of daisies. She looked wonderful. Gert was in a white tuxedo and all his anger was gone. Their countenances were shining with a heavenly light. Your sister, Margareta was standing by watching them. She put her arms around them both and I think they are all at peace now."

Maisie took both Helen's hands in hers and squeezed tight. "What a wonderful gift you have my dear. You have brought relief to a grieving old lady. Thank you."

Helen offered to drive Maisie back to the hotel. Wisp settled in Maisie's lap as they drove in silence.

Maisie went off to her room to pack her bags and left after breakfast the next morning. Mr. van Rooyen offered them a free weekend accommodation any time they wanted it but they knew they would never return.

Helen and Ada bid them farewell and promised to visit. Maisie assured them of a warm welcome if they were ever to be in the district and they swapped phone numbers and addresses. They stood on the driveway watching as the little car disappeared into a cloud of dust.

Helen also returned to her room to pack. Their holiday over and reality seemed almost surreal compared to the last two weeks.

The next night at their home in Pietermaritzburg, Gordon came around for a visit. Helen felt her heart flip in her chest as he leaned in to give her a peck on the cheek. He brought a large bouquet of flowers for Ada. Helen put them in a vase and the three of them were soon sitting outside in the garden with tall glasses of icy juice.

Helen had baked a lemon cake which Gordon made short work of. "So, Bell ladies, I never did find out what transpired in Bulwer. Come on, spill the beans. I told you not to investigate the murder, but I have a sneaky feeling you ignored my advice."

"Nothing much. We found out Maisie was indeed, Charlotte's mother. But she had nothing to do with her daughter's death. It turns out Charlotte had taken the knobkerrie from Mr. van Rooyen's office herself and someone had turned it on her. Let's just say it was all resolved," Helen admitted.

Gordon looked over at Helen and winked at her as he thought of the secret they shared with Maisie. "Yes, I suppose it was all resolved in its own way. Do you know an old Zulu lady told me once that the ancestors would solve the murder and that I must focus on affairs of the heart. At the time I didn't want to listen but maybe she was not so crazy after all?"

Ada leaned forward and refilled his glass. "Justice was done and restitution was made. And it is the end of it young man. The good Lord will judge those he will judge and who are we to question his ways?"

Helen leaned back in her chair and asked how Gordon's day had been. Ada excused herself and went to see how dinner was cooking. Wisp jumped up on Helen's lap and then, as if noticing Gordon for the first time, she changed allegiance and laps. "Sorry Gordon, she does love to drop her fur on a good uniform or suit when she is offered the chance. Here let me take her off you."

Helen leaned over Gordon to pick up the cat when he gently pulled her down onto his lap. Wisp jumped off in disgust, but neither of the humans noticed her departure. Gordon twirled a curl of Helen's hair around his finger as he looked deep into her eyes.

"Helen, I could never replace David in your affections, but do you think you could find a small corner of your heart just for me?"

Helen didn't say a thing as she looked down into his eyes and into the depths of his soul. She touched his lips with her fingers and thought it had been a while since she had dreamed of David and now the man haunting her dreams belonged to this precious face in front of her.

"Oh, I think I can find a small corner or two somewhere. Maybe if you tried really hard we could even find a spot in the sunlight. Because, yes, you have invaded my heart and mind, my dreams and my imaginings. David would be happy for us. I think he might even be instrumental in manipulating the fates to get us together," Helen said breathlessly as she snuggled onto his lap and slipped her hand under his jacket to caress his chest.

Gordon smiled as he pulled her closer still and kissed her forehead and then allowed his lips to travel down her face. She moaned in pleasure when his lips found   hers.

HISTORICAL NOTES

Mountain Park Hotel is real and is still in business in Bulwer, South Africa. It was built in 1940 by Italian prisoners of war during World War 11. The hotel is known as one of the most haunted hotels in South Africa and often hosts murder mystery weekends. The ghosts include the original owner, Mr. McMenigel who died in a suspicious house fire that could have been a suicide after he went bankrupt before the hotel was completed. There is also a small girl called Mathilda who is seen sitting with her head in her hands and her school desk is often moved by ghostly hands when she is not happy with its situation. A small white dog named Wisp is also seen trotting along the passageways. The author has taken liberties with the floor plan and some of the rooms are not where they should be and added extra ghosts to enhance the story line. Charlotte is one of the listed ghosts and is supposed to have fallen to her death after an argument with a soldier on the third floor. The author has adapted the death to suit her story.

South Africa took part in World War 11 with 334,000 volunteers taking part. 211,000 White South Africans along with 77,000 Africans and 46,000 mixed race soldiers fought in the Desert War, Italian Campaign, Madagascar, Warsaw and Japan. The RAF had bases along the coast of South Africa to combat enemy activity. South Africa lost 11,000 soldiers during the war and the Commonwealth War Graves list them in their archives. There was no conscription due to the fact that the Boer contingent did not want to support the British as feelings were still sensitive because of the Boer war at the beginning of the century. The age of enlistment was supposed to be twenty but many young men, including the father of the author, enlisted at a younger age.

Perla Gibson is historically correct. She was an opera singer that was known for her singing to the troop ships as they left Durban harbour. Perla would sing through a megaphone to the departing and returning soldiers even on the very day that she received the news that her own son had been killed in the war. Soldiers especially enjoyed her rendition of 'When Irish eyes are smiling'. Many soldiers had no family or friends to farewell them at the port and her presence gave them a sense of motherly love and concern. She became a competent artist and often attended shows around the country (where the author met her in the 1960's). Perla would display her artwork and disperse sound advice to those willing to listen. When the author was eight years old Perla advised her to 'remember to paint the negative spaces as well as the positive ones.' This advice has stayed with the author all her life and has influenced her style of painting. Perla did wear a large floppy hat and loved helping other artists to hone their skills. As far as we know she did not have a workshop at Reichnau Mission but it is feasible that she ran artists retreats during her lifetime.

Reichnau Mission was established in 1886 and run by Trappist monks. It sits alongside the Pelola River and features a school, butchery and bakery. Forge around the Gothic style church with its beautiful murals and stained-glass windows. Trappists believe in self-sufficiency and have maintained the mission for over 130 years. The school, church and mill are still in use today. The mission is situated about 15 km outside Underberg in the Drakensberg mountain range of South Africa.

The Yellowwood Church is a small church standing behind a lynch gate and was built in 1885 on the outskirts of Bulwer. It has stood the test of time and is a beautiful simple chapel that has a deep spiritual ambience to it. Over time it has become disused and neglected in parts. The graves between the lynch gate and the chapel are in various stages of decay. The roof has been replaced with green corrugated iron to prevent further damage to the inside. From its grounds you get a view of the Amahaqwa mountain which rises up behind the Mountain Park Hotel.

ISBN Paperback: 978-0-473-45259-9
ISBN Epub: 978-0-473-45260-5